the illusion of movement

To Esther with love

Peter Raposo

Peter Raposo

APS Books
Yorkshire

APS Books,
The Stables Field Lane, Aberford, West Yorkshire, LS25 3AE

APS Books is a subsidiary of the
APS Publications imprint

www.andrewsparke.com

First published worldwide by APS Books in 2021

Love dies…

Here we go…

Love dies. I have no doubt about it. Sadly, I've seen it happening; I've seen love die, turn itself into hate, vicious hate, vicious lies, a hate even stronger than the love that had just died.

Love dies and becomes something else. At times, it becomes the opposite of what it used to be; it becomes hate, other times it becomes pain, an endless pain, a pain that can lead the loser into a dark path, a pain that becomes a dark path, a pain that consumes you from within, eats you away slowly, a pain that, if you're not strong enough, it can kill you.

When you killed our love and sent me away, I retreated into a dark corner, a corner from which I thought there was no escape. I saw myself walking in the woods, losing myself in the dark woods, go down on my knees, commit hara-kiri, as if I was some lonely samurai who was punishing myself for my wrongdoings, but I had done nothing wrong, apart from loving too much, working too much, being faithful, bowing to every wish of yours. In return, you paid me with betrayal, a heartless betrayal, not with another man but with lies, and when I wasn't looking (because I was too tired), you took everything, including our children, everything and so much more, and you told everyone that I was the one who had done wrong, that I never did enough for you at home, that I was lazy, useless, and I saw too late that you were a liar, but you can't even tell that you're lying. In fact, I believe that you're not well in the head; you seem to think that the world is against you, that everyone is whispering about you, that the Universe is against you. You want for everyone to stop what they're doing and listen to you, follow the same religion as you, worship you, lift you up and praise you to the stars, but you've lied!

You've lied to yourself, to the Universe.

You've gone against Nature. What chance do you think you have?

Love dies. I know it does. I've seen you killing it.

1

Love dies and one of the partners turns into a snake. Sometimes both partners can turn into snakes. Luckily I didn't, but your poison almost killed me.

Love dies. Just live with it, but don't live with the pain.

The pain can kill you.

Leave it behind.

Leave it and wait.

Don't pursue what you can't catch.

Leave it and wait.

Don't chase those who didn't want you.

Leave them behind.

Love dies and it becomes some sort of ghost, or some dishonourable creature that chases you in your dreams, a ghost-like feeling that turns the brightness you once had in your life into darkness, and the killer of love doesn't care if you either live or die. The killer of love only cares about what it can get from you.

My killer wants money.

It took everything from me, including the car and children, left me with nothing, and now it wants more money.

Money…

Love dies and turns into greed.

My love is still alive. I'm not greedy. Or maybe I am. Maybe I want too much: too much love, a bit of it, just a hug, someone to love, someone that cares, someone that is honest and truthful. Yes, I am greedy.

My love is still alive, waiting for the right person, waiting.

Love dies and turns into an episode of Oprah. Both partners run to the show, tell their version of it, or maybe one of us keeps quiet about it or says little about it.

Poor Oprah nods her head and thinks, "What shall I do? Who can I believe?"

Oprah becomes our priest. One of us confesses our failures, pain and hopes to her while the other simply lies. But maybe the liar believes her own lie.

I'll write my version of it, the testimony of the one who walked through the darkness and pain and almost lost it all, but maybe I'm wrong. After all, I'm not perfect, and lately I've realised that you're suffering too, but your pain comes from the fact that you're not getting what you want. But what do you want? More money? I'm sorry but I'm poor.

Maybe I'm being unfair.

Maybe you want love too but you don't know where to look for it.

Love dies.

Can you resurrect yours?

I hope you can.

I see you years from now looking for me, or, worse, living with regret.

Regret is a terrible feeling. It eats you inside, and you only realise that you're living with it years down the road, when it's already too late.

And it's already too late, for both of us, because I no longer love you.

For now, because of them, because of our children, you must remain a part of my life, and so, for now, as everything becomes clear and a new dawn starts, I must have a bit of darkness in my life, just a tiny bit, but I must not let it consume me and eat away the bit of hope that I have.

Love dies.

How sad.

Thank God mine is still alive.

I'm going to hold on to it like a precious treasure, treasure my treasure, and then give it to someone special.

Better luck next time, I hope.

For me, and for you, too.

The Snake

The bus drives past me and I keep on walking. It is a forty minute walk to town. I could have caught the bus and be there in less than 15 minutes but a long walk will be good for me. It is therapeutic, good for the soul and the body. It allows me to think and to exercise. Lately I've been thinking too much, but what is there to think about? A person thinks about the past, wondering why this or that happened, why didn't things happen differently, why weren't we given better chances, better choices, better this, better that, instead of nothing, but things have a reason for being, life knows what it is doing, and the wanna-be poet must take everything that comes his or her way with a silly smile on its face.

In 2005 I found myself back in London, ready to realise my dreams, ready to love, ready to fall in love again. One week in my city of birth, I saw a new dawn, the chance for a new beginning, but had I known then what I know now I would have run away from the snake in front of me, a snake in the shape of a woman; Lilith in the Garden of Eden. On that tragic morning (but I didn't know yet the pain that the beast would bring into my life) she had a big smile on her face and she spoke like an angel, but she was trying to run away from her imaginative demons (later, I too would become one of those imaginative demons that she created in that childish, cruel mind of hers), trying to find a poor sucker (yes, I suck –and I sucked her well, too; not that I mind that bit) that would rescue her from her imaginative trials, and so I took on that role, the role of the hero, the foolish hero, a hero that would be sent on a loveless journey that would last close to sixteen years, a cold journey where the floors were a cold marble and the walls were made of ice, a journey that mighty Vikings would be too scared to take, a journey where I became some sort of Odysseus and she, my soon to be wife Yu, became a student of Calypso.

We met in February 2005, a few days after my 32nd birthday, a few days after I had escaped depression, a failed suicide attempt, and Death – maybe Hell, too. Needless to say, after having left my Personal Hell behind, I was ready to start a new life. Instead I was given a snake for a wife. Oh, look; I'm starting to rhyme. How ironic seeing that, once upon a time, I used to be a lame poet.

Ah, the games that Life likes to play with us. But I can't complain (or can I?); after all, I needed some inspiration for some new stories, inspiration for madness, madness to create, and so Life laughed at me and said, "I'll give you this: love, pain, heartache, and more madness. Make of it what you will."

And then Death laughed at me and said, "You won't escape Me this time. I'll make you go through Hell, again. And this time the pain will be deeper. And then you will be Mine."

Ah, Life and Death playing chess, me in the middle, the last pawn left, being flicked around, to the edge, to the dawn, losing my mind, wondering which way to go. Could Kelly Howell and her meditation save me? Could I go deep enough and save myself? Yes, of course.

You no longer need Love.

Love is a lie, created by Man, perfected by Woman.

She deceives you with her tongue, with her round breasts, her perfect feet, her beautiful legs, her sex, and you go down, all the way down, until you're completely lost, absorbed by the Lie, a Lie you call Love, a lie created by Man, perfected by Woman, lost in that Garden, her Garden, a hairy Garden but later she will shave it off.

She becomes your Muse, your Everything, and then she takes Everything, leaving you with Nothing.

That is Love, her way of loving.

She goes down on you, All the Way Down, right to your balls.

She conquers you with her tongue, with her legs, with her vagina, with Love, but Love is a Lie, a Lie that she perfected.

What chance do you have against that magnificent Tongue of hers, a Tongue that tells you sweet words and goes All the Way Down, right to your Balls?

Splat…

You come and she smiles.

She has conquered you.
You love her.

Once in town, I sit somewhere, alone, away from everyone, and I write.

I'm writing a novel, a crap sci-fi novel about Love, the Loss of Love, lockdowns, face masks, an Invisible Enemy, Lies, Love, the Loss of Everything.

A memoir?

NOOOOO?!

Maybe…

I'll turn the memoir into a Lie, turn it into Fiction, a fictional tale of liars, blowjobs, cunnilingus, asexuality, tears, and I might even add aliens to it. A space opera with Mickey Rourke and Kim Basinger as the main characters, fighting aliens, making love and lying. The Villain will be a virus, an Invisible Enemy, and those who sell fear for a living. Or, the villain will be various people; villains. One of them will be an evil geeky billionaire who thinks of himself as some sort of scientist and saviour of the world, and he will want us to eat synthetic meat and insects while he eats the best of foods. And he will be friends with another billionaire, some evil guy called Jeff, a child molester, killed in jail, murdered by an ex-President and his evil wife, or by some killer hired by them, and then the media, controlled by some of the villains, will tell us that it was suicide. And later, the killer of Jeff, will die because of some virus. Case closed. Yes, maybe I should write that novel.

I'm going slightly crazy. Ever since Yu asked for the divorce I've been losing my mind, writing the weirdest of stuff. Henry Miller's *Tropic of Cancer* comes to mind as I sit on the steps of a closed church looking at the notebook in front of me. Miller too went crazy, and then he wrote all those magnificent books. He needed a Muse to write. Pain became his muse.

Yes, I've finally solved the greatest mystery of all, the answer to "What is Love?"

Love is pain.

There you go.

Mystery solved.

During lockdown, while everything was shut, empty parks and the steps of closed churches became my refuge, a refuge for the lost poet, the failed poet, a memoirist travelling through the Dark Night of the Soul, down that abyss called Depression, a memoirist turned novelist, a broken man, lost and alone, no longer living with his children, a dreamer living in a nightmare, losing his faith, talking to himself, talking to the skies, asking Someone, "Why did You forsake me? Why did You abandon me? Why?"

I stood outside churches, looking around me, looking at a cross, at the walls, at the emptiness of my soul, the emptiness of my life, at the squirrels running past me, pigeons staring at me, two ducks walking past me, I kid you not, and I went crazy.

I became like the character of Shun Kaidou a.k.a. Jet-Black Wings, a hero fighting an evil conspiracy organization called Dark Reunion, but the evil conspiracy organization that I was fighting (in vain because I could never defeat them on my own) really exists and it is called The Invisible Hand. It exists, doesn't it? It does... and it controls everything. And they're probably paying me to write this.

And afterwards I became like Rimbaud, a young Rimbaud walking through the streets of Paris, a young poet lost in the madness that is this world, and everywhere I went, everyone was wearing face masks, and the moment they saw me, wearing no mask, walking towards them, they would cross the road running, or they would jump and try to merge in with the walls around them. The Fear was real. The Fear of the Invisible Enemy, a virus that no one was allowed to say out loud lest we were demonetized or/and pursued by the media and the law and everyone else that works for the Invisible Hand.

The world became dumb, deaf and blind, and during that time, while everyone was living inside the biggest prison of all, a prison of the mind, a brainless prison, a prison where different ideas and opinions weren't allowed to be shared, the Invisible Hand filled its already fat coffins with more money. But they want more, so much more, even our souls, and so this Invisible Enemy keeps on living, mutating by the month, and the people are given short breaks, and allowed to do a bit more (but not much more), and the Invisible Leader says that it is for their best that they're living in the widest prison of all. Not only that, everyone must get vaccinated, because the Invisible Hand really cares for the people, and while the people cower and nod and clap Stupidity, the Invisible Hand travels the world on holidays, go to football matches, eat the best of foods, catch up on their suntans, and the little people are told that they must not travel and that, later, maybe they would have to eat insects. And the people nod and clap while the Invisible Hand laughs its head off.

And while I was going crazy, the Snake was enjoying her life in her new home, a home paid, in part, by my sweat. And the reason why the Snake had a job to pay her mortgage was because I found her one, but the moment she had everything she needed from me, she asked for the divorce and set off to her Counterfeit Paradise while leaving me alone in the Darkness.

I died.

Love died.

I actually died.

Something inside me died.

I went through my own Dark Night of the Soul.

I cried so much.

I cried for days, weeks, months.

After a while, I could no longer cry.

I was ready to die. Again.

I even arranged the place and the time and the method of death. But it never came. Because…

One day I entered a church, and in there I found Jesus, and when I felt His presence around me, I started to cry. And I heard a voice from within say, "Love isn't dead. It's just waiting for the right time to resurrect. Hang in there. Don't carry the cross. I carried it for you. Now hang in there for just a bit longer."

I cried for a bit longer. And then I decided to live. And to write. Keep a journal. Write and live. Live to write.

And while I was writing, the Snake was laughing. But one day we all have to answer for our deeds, either here or in the world to come. And sometimes, while we're still in this world, Karma and Nature join hands with Payback, and Life becomes a Bitch.

I tried. You lied. And I almost died

And even after you lied, in your own mind (but how?) (really?), you still believed you were right and that you were allowed to lie and hurt whoever got in your way.

You took everything. Everything and a bit more.

And you lied even more.

And you kept on lying because, by then, the lie had taken over you.

Suddenly, because of your lie, I became the bad guy.

But one day your lie will be exposed. How will you live with yourself then?

I say nothing. Instead I write this.

But this is nothing, not even a lie. I will just call if fiction.

Not so long ago, in this galaxy...

So, diary time.

I'll have to lie and call it fiction, because, you know, just in case...

I'll date some bits just so you know who you are. But first, let me put this Genet book away, on top of that Sara Maitland and Ma Jian books. After the breakout, I gave a lot of my books away, but I kept a few, because, you know, I like books. But the Snake hated the fact that I like books. Hmm, strange woman.

21-2-2021

A cold loveless world, a world where no one seems to love the person close to them. G-d has closed his eyes, or so some people say, and forgotten about us. What now?

Asteroid Apophis is on the way. Some people are scared, saying that Apophis could destroy satellites and spaceships.

Another apocalypse.

We seem to get one every year but nothing ever seems to happen. Then again, last year was a bit crazy. And this year isn't getting any better.

And then you have the news; Right and Left, and even the Centre, all selling Fear, because Fear sells.

Fear is like a drug. Everyone wants a taste of it; don't deny it.

Last year, the world closed down, all because of a virus. But the lockdown(s) didn't stop the people from dying. And it didn't kill the virus. And I shouldn't be writing this because nowadays we're only allowed to write a few things and not everything. We're not even allowed to mention the virus by its name on YouTube and other online pages or else…who knows?

Last year was a crazy year, and the craziness extended itself to this year. Last year…

There are days when I can only write about last year on the third person.

Last year, in a galaxy not far away, a man lost everything and almost went crazy.

Last year his wife asked for the divorce. He'd seen it coming miles away.

He'd seen it coming yet he stood still, waiting for the pain to arrive.

What else could he do but wait?

A cold loveless world…

He reads what he just wrote. This morning, after he finished work, he walked all the way home. A long tiring walk but he wanted to walk, to be done with his thoughts (but he spends a lot of time on his own, alone with his thoughts, so why walk all the way home when he could catch the bus?). For the last few weeks, because of this never-ending lockdown (it was only supposed to last a month, if that, but, a year later, the lockdown shows no sign of coming to an end although, rumour has it, they're talking about bringing it to an end by next month – by now, some politicians and billionaires have become even richer while the poor have become poorer), he's been spending a lot of time at his ex-wife's new place, a place that she bought behind is back (but that's another story, and he already wrote about; memoirs which he then turned into a long sci-fi novel).

At first, his ex-wife didn't want him inside her home, but not so long ago she had a change of mind and she told him he could go to her place every day if he wants to, and she even offered him a key for her place. But he said no. And no.

She wants me back but I won't go back to her.

She doesn't know what she wants.

Sometimes she wants Heaven, sometimes she wants Hell.

She better be careful because she might get what she wants. But she doesn't know what she wants.

On the way home he listened to Arvo Part's *Da Pacem* on his iPhone. Deserted streets. The world was sleeping. Not a single walker on sight. The world was scared. Later, at the park, he saw a woman walking her dog. He missed having a woman by his side but could he love again? Would he trust again?

There was another woman after the breakup, last year, a woman named Brie. They went out for almost three months. He was still living with his ex (legally, she wasn't yet his ex, but their marriage had ended years ago), just waiting for her new home to be ready, but on the same day that he moved out of the apartment that he shared with his ex, he also broke up with Brie. Something inside him had died. Something was broken and he needed to be alone.

He told Brie he wasn't ready for another relationship. Not yet. Not so soon.

He just wanted to be left alone and cry, but he didn't tell this to Brie. And maybe Brie was the right one (but she wasn't; in his heart, he knew that she wasn't the one).

He broke up with her and went somewhere else to cry, into a dark corner of his soul. And maybe Brie cried too. Of course she cried, but he couldn't love her. And he couldn't lie.

He's now renting a small bedroom in the middle of nowhere, living alone, starting again with nothing, starting a new life at the age of 49-years old. It's not too late to start again; it's never too late to start again, is it? – but it's fair to say that he's a bit scared of the future. Then again, during these troubled times, who isn't?

He sits on the carpeted floor, his back resting against his bed. He misses his children. He misses what he's losing; their smiles, a few jokes, their laughter, small moments that he will never see, moments that he can't relive. He's missing and sometimes he feels like dying.

A few hours' sleep out of the way, he meditates for a few minutes.

A friend once told him, "The Lord's with you, every step of the way. He's there for you when you fall, ready to catch you, lift you up, and teach you how to fly."

And then he's out of the door, another long walk, his destination unknown. He grabs a cup of coffee and a tuna sandwich from a local shop, sits somewhere, alone, masticates on his food, swallows his drink, reads a few chapters of a Kabbalistic book, wonders how his children are, puffs, puffs away, sighs, and waits.

He waits on another day, another chance but **Where's G-d? Give me a break. Another chance. Please.**

He puffs, sighs, pleads, and waits.

A long wait.

Sometimes he feels like dying.

Sometimes he feels as if he's dying.

A breakup isn't just a breakup.

A breakup is the tearing of a heart.

Sometimes, the death of a soul.

His friend Saul wants to write a book. A Young Adult Novel. Something along the lines of J. K. Rowling, but a bit more serious, with a few elements of Kabbalah, so that children can take something from the book, learn something from it. Saul is a teacher, a taught mind, but, so far, apart from the author and a few friends, he has no students.

M÷, the author of this book, listens to his friend and nods.

M÷ has written a few books and Saul wants some guidance on how to write a book, but M÷ doesn't know what to say.

"Just write," M÷ says. What else can he say?

Saul shrugs his shoulders. "But where do I start?" he asks.

"At the beginning," M÷ says. "And, because it will be your book, only you know where the beginning is."

What else can he say?

They sit on Saul's old sofa, a sofa covered on cat hair. There's coffee and a tray of biscuits in front of them. Lots of books around them as Saul reads as much as M÷.

Saul has a house, a family, a plan, something, while M÷ is still looking for something. Again.

His search never seems to end and he's getting a bit tired, not to mention depressed.

Not so long ago he used to have something, and he was trying to achieve a bit more, but then came the breakup, the betrayal, the kick. His ex-wife didn't betray him with another man. She betrayed him with scorn and coldness.

One day the tables will turn.
One day you will know how I feel.
One day you will pay.
Are you ready for that day?
You aren't…

How can you prepare for the end?
How do you prepare for pain?

And while M÷ is renting a small bedroom in the middle of nowhere, his ex-wife Yu bought her own place, a two-bedroom maisonette. A small home, no place in it for M÷, not even a photo of him lying around. He has no photos of Yu at his place either. She's a snake. Why would he want to look at a snake?

A few weeks before they went their separate ways, he gave her most of the photos where they were together. She could do whatever she wanted with them. He didn't care. Other photos he simply chucked in the bin. He even went through some of his USB sticks and deleted some of Yu's photos but kept the ones where she was with their children.

Did he hate her?

Did he hate Yu?

No.

Yes…

He never hated anyone, not even those who hurt him, not even those who bullied him and almost drove him to suicide, but now he's finally learning how to hate. Maybe he needed to learn how to hate.

His father once told him, "You're too good."

Saul once told him, "You're too good."

Too good was another way of them saying, "You're too soft. Weak."

No more.

Now it was time to hate, hate just a bit, and the best way to hate those who hurt him is by ignoring them. And so he ignores them.

The phone rings. He ignores it.

They text him. He ignores them.

Life goes on.

He must move on, again, with noting, without Yu, without that lying snake. Maybe life isn't that bad.

He used to go to a synagogue but the synagogues are now closed. Last year, for some reason, he heard a voice inside of him telling to look for

Yeshua ben Yosef, or Iêsous, better known as Jesus. One morning, face mask on, he entered Coventry Cathedral, and when he saw the large tapestry Christ in Glory in the Tetramorph, he found himself crying in the middle of the cathedral, crying in front of everyone (but there weren't that many people inside the cathedral; only eight or nine people, if that), and he felt so weak and sad and lost as he looked at that magnificent work of art. Not only that, he also felt something inside of him, something unexplainable, and he felt a voice coming from within him, telling him to be patient; be patient and wait: "stand still and put your faith in the Lord," that voice inside of him said.

And so he sat down.

And cried.

Psalm 37:7

Not so long ago his ex-wife Yu had some problems at work, this at a time when she was already living at her new place while M÷, the (sometimes) narrator of this, was living in a small bedroom. Okay, the bedroom wasn't that small, but it wasn't big enough for him to have his children living with him. Anyway, going back to the snake known as Yu; she had some problems at work (for the record, she's working at the same place as M÷, and the only reason why she got the job was because M÷ spoke with the manager and told her, the manager, that he had someone for the position of receptionist, or admin, since there were two positions available at work, and Drew, the manager, said, "Tell her to come and see me," and M÷ told Yu about the job, or jobs if you prefer, a job she badly needed because she had quit her last job, and the one before that, and the one before that, and now she couldn't find any work; needless to say, she got the job, and once she started that job, she started to plan a new life, a new life for her, a life without M÷, a selfish life, a selfish plan, a selfish home for her selfish self, which was nothing new (for as long as M÷ has known her, 16 years and counting, Yu always had problems at work, and ever since he has known her, 16 years and counting, she's quit almost every single job she's had because someone said something or someone did something or whatever), and now, because she had some problems at work, she wanted M÷ next to her, and she wanted for him to hear her, and help her if needed, and, just in case she lost her job, could he please pay for

17

her mortgage and bills, "which isn't a lot," she said, but once she got back on her feet could he please PISS OFF!!!

She didn't say those words but she might as well have said them.

She was a snake, and snakes are dangerous.

She was a snake but she thought of herself as the victim, or, worse, as an angel. But wasn't the Snake a fallen angel? Sssssssssssssssssssss.

M÷ spent a few nights at her place but they slept in separate beds, and one night, she asked him, "Why didn't you fight for our marriage?"

Once again she was playing the victim. Had she forgotten that she started to plan for a life without him behind his back, while they were still married?

Had she forgotten how she was constantly bullying him, telling him to move out, find a room and move out, take nothing and give her everything?

M÷ said, "I told you to wait, think things through, don't destroy the family, but you didn't listen to a word I said."

That shut her up.

What could she say when she knew he was right?

He stayed at her place for a few days, cooked for the family, every day, every night, ironed the clothes; their clothes, not his, but one afternoon, as it often happened, Yu snapped, and, once again, showed her true self and called him useless, pathetic, and whatever, and M÷ saw that she was only using him, as she often did, and that he could never love someone like her. No wonder her own family kept away from her.

M÷ said, "You're always using me. You only care for yourself. Lately, because you had problems at work, you wanted me here, but now that everything is better, you've gone back to your cold self."

He put on his shoes, grabbed his bag, kissed his children goodbye, and left her place.

He could no longer be in the same room as Yu. She was poison.

He made his way to the bus stop, cursing under his breath, cursing but why? He was tired of it all. That's why.

Tired of lies, tired of being used, tired of everything, tired of having nothing.

The love he felt for Yu had officially been dead for a long time but she was making him hate her even more.

Ever since he was a child (a baby!!!), he kept being pushed around, from house to house, sometimes from city to city, and he was tired of it all.

He stood by the bus stop thinking about his life.

"What a shitty life," he thought.

When he was only a baby, his parents had left him with a cold woman. Decades later, he married (and divorced) another cold woman. All his brothers and sister were more or less settled down, had their own partners, a place to call home, someone by their side, while M÷ was still being pushed around. Well, it was his turn to stop being pushed around. It was his turn to go cold. Become cold.

He sat on the bus reading Bolaño's *Amulet*. The bus was empty. Only him and the driver.

Minimal traffic on the roads. Nevertheless the bus driver drove slowly. He had a schedule, hardly a soul waiting.

M÷ kept on reading. He read to forget.

He read for inspiration.

Bolaño was one of his heroes, not to mention the author of *The Savage Detectives*, M÷'s favourite book of all time. Too bad Mr Bolaño lived a short life. It's fair to say that Bolaño was only getting started before Death took him away at the age of 50-years old.

When M÷ got to the city centre, seeing that it was too early for he to go to work, he sat somewhere, reading, contemplating his thoughts, thinking about tomorrow.

Tomorrow…

Thinking about the past, about 1999, about a crazy woman he had, about a woman, someone, someone to love, someone…

1999. A pub in Hammersmith. A cool evening. A busy night at the bar.

Achy's already drunk, not to mention high.

I'm not drinking alcohol and I haven't had a joint yet. I like to smoke weed when I'm indoors, hidden from the world. That way I won't make a fool of myself in front of others.

Achy's body seems to be turning green. She looks me in the eye and says, really loudly, "I want you to come home with me and suck my pussy."

She says it loud, really loud.

A few faces stare at us.

I see their eyes on us. I feel them. I see them all and feel it all.

Achy can't see a thing, only lust.

"Come on. Let's leave this *mierda* and go back to my place. Time for your dinner, baby. Time for some *coño*," says Achy.

And this is why I don't smoke weed when I'm out

Notes.

Notes everywhere.
Notes for nothing.
Notes about nothing.
Notes that he has kept for decades.
Not so long ago he started to use some of his old notes as ideas for some of his stories.
Not so long ago his wife asked him for a divorce.
Not so long ago, he had to start again, with nothing, aged 49.
Scary times for him, but he must go on. If not, what else can he do?

The world, before the Invisible Enemy

I was sitting in the same insane old black room; the dark room of my childhood, now the dark room of my adulthood. A dark room in a dark house. A dark house stinking of sweat, piss, mould and bleach. My palace of nightmares, I called it. Or, the cemetery of dead dreams.

It was a place like no other, an infernal palace, and I had no Beatrice to guide me out of there, to lead me out of the darkness.

I had no plans for the night, no books to read, and I couldn't turn the lights on and write for a bit.

I felt depressed as hell.

I still had my clothes on. Dressed, with nowhere to go.

Grandmother was still awake, lying in bed in her dark room, a room stinking of piss and sweat. She had a bucket under her bed which she used to piss on. Disgusting. And the room stank, so badly, of piss and sweat. Then, in the morning (but not every morning), she would empty the bucket in the toilet. And the toilet was a dump, same as the entire house, even the kitchen. Nothing worked. Everything was falling apart. You would use the toilet, have a dump, and afterwards you wouldn't be able to flush it out because the toilet didn't work properly. You would have to get a bucket of water and pour it over the shit. A horrible place, I'm telling you.

I was in my bedroom, wondering, wanting to die. Grandmother was still awake, spitting, waiting, listening in the dark, spying, always spying. Yes, that house was a palace of nightmares. Or a cemetery of dead dreams. The longer I stayed in there the closer I was to become a dead dreamer. And the end almost came but I was saved. And I already wrote about it, another book, maybe a few books, the same old boring story.

Grandmother was listening, to me, to everything. She knew I was still awake. And she probably knew I was depressed but she didn't care. She thought of my depression as weakness. A weakness. And Grandmother was strong, as strong as a demon.

I looked out of the window and I looked at the time. The moon and the stars were my light.

The moon and the stars were my witnesses, the witnesses to the insanity that was my life. But was life that bad? It was.

Imagine living in a house where you're not allowed to have the lights on, and you can't read or write when you dream of becoming an author. Imagine seeing your dreams disappear, your hope being crushed, your heart being stabbed, slowly, every single night. And little by little, your little eyes start to widen but your vision deteriorates. With time, even though you can still see, you learn how to move in the dark. You become a bat but someone else is sucking your blood, destroying your dreams, watching your soul weakening.

Was life that bad?

You tell me.

A few minutes past 9PM. Still early. Back then I used to go to bed quite late. Nowadays, if I can, I'm in bed by 8PM.

I looked around me, at the darkness in that room, heard Grandmother coughing, and thought of what to do.

I couldn't sleep. Not in that house.

I couldn't dream. Not in that house.

How could I dream when I was living in a nightmare?

For years, I slept so badly in that house, sometimes for less than five hours a day, every single day, sleeping less and less, every single day, living in a nightmare, living a nightmare, every single day, a nightmare. *The last years with Yu weren't much better as I slept even less than at Grandmother's house.*

I thought about going to Porta Velha in Travessa Manuel Dias Barão. I liked it there. It was a quiet place where I could drink a cup of coffee, a glass of wine, smoke my cigarettes without being bothered, and write for a bit in a lightened room.

My mind was already made up (I was going to Porta Velha), but as I reached for my notebook my mobile phone rang. I looked at the number. It was my friend Luis. One of my best friends. I reached for the phone, answered it, and heard Luis say, "Hey, are you home?"

"Yes," I said.

"What are you doing tonight?" he asked.

"Not much," I said.

"I'm arriving in Largo Gil Eanes soon. Meet me there if you want to go somewhere, have some fun," he said.

"Sure. Give me five minutes," I said. And, just like that, a night out was planned.

Throughout the years, while living in Portimão, I would meet with a lot of my friends at Largo Gil Eanes, and then we would head off somewhere else. That's what happened on that night.

I grabbed my notebook, a pack of cigarettes, a couple of pens, put on my shoes, and left the room.

A dark corridor in front of me but I already knew my way in the dark.

Grandmother was still awake, listening, always listening. Listening to me walking along the corridor, listening to me going down the steps, listening to me walking in the dark; in that house I always made my way in the dark. Walking in the dark, blinking my tired eyes, walking, blinking, hoping. And once I was out of the cemetery of dead dreams, I saw light in the street. And I felt someone watching me, an eerie presence nearby. I didn't have to look up to know that Grandmother was watching me from behind the curtains in her smelly bedroom. In fact, I didn't dare to look up and see those eyes hiding in the dark, watching me.

I made my way down Rua Dona Maria Luísa, and I was glad to be out of that infernal house, glad to see a bit of light around me.

My life then was a constant road to nowhere. Bad decisions had been made by me when I was a young man (but, in my defence, I didn't have anyone to guide me, to teach me better), and now, because of it, I was suffering. But I could still change. And I could still achieve something.

23

My friend Luis was already at Largo Gil Eanes waiting for me. I saw him sitting on a bench, smoking, looking as if he didn't have a care in the whole world. He got up when he saw me approaching and smiled. It was a cool evening and there were lots of people in the park, sitting on benches, smoking, talking, or heading to the nearest café.

We shook hands, greeted one another, and afterwards Luis said, "Hey, do you want to go to Lisbon?"

"What? Tonight?" I asked.

"Yeah, man. I'm meeting Paulo there and then I'm bringing him back to Portimão sometime tomorrow," said Luis.

Paulo was a good friend of ours and he was Luis' best friend. They had known one another since primary school.

I looked at my watch. It was 9:16PM. It was still early, but not that early, especially to go on a road trip to Lisbon.

"What time do you think we'll get to Lisbon?" I asked.

"Oh, before midnight. And then we can rest at Paulo's place, spend a few hours in Lisbon, and drive back after lunch," Luis said.

That sounded like a good idea.

I said okay.

We arrived in Lisbon after 5AM.

What happened was we stopped in Faro to see some friends. Afterwards a few joints were passed around, everyone got the munchies, then we went somewhere to eat, junk food, of course, got talking for a long time, smoked a few cigarettes, drank a few espressos, and then we got back in the car. I don't even know what time we left Faro but it was late, really late, and by the time we got to Lisbon Paulo was already up, waiting for us. His uncle was in Manchester, England, visiting some family, and the apartment where Paulo was staying belonged to his uncle. It was a large apartment, the kind of place where I could see myself living for the rest of my life, a proper home for a writer. The living room was crowded by bookshelves. Books right up to the ceiling. Books on the floor. Books on top of a desk facing a large window.

"My dream home," I thought.

Needless to say, both Luis and I were tired but we still managed to talk for a bit with Paulo before retreating to bed. We slept in Paulo's bedroom. Luis slept in a sleeping bag while I slept on Paulo's bed. As for Paulo, since he was already up, he stayed in the living room. He went out for a bit while we were sleeping, just to a café around the corner. Later, I found out that he was reading a book of poems by Herberto Hélder. He gave me that book. That alone was worth the trip.

6th March 2021

He took the day off just so he could spend some time with his children but he made sure to tell in advance to Yu that he was booking the day off. Her mood varied from day to day, sometimes from minute to minute; one minute she was warm, then, seconds later, she was cold and cruel. Depending on the day, or on the mood, M÷ never knew what type of Yu he would get. As time went by he was coming to the conclusion that the divorce had been a blessing.

One morning he called to let her know that he was booking the day off and gave her the date. Yu was in a good mood and said, "Okay. You can come here and even stay the night with the children. They would love that. They always want to spend the day with you."

He thanked her.

"Happy days," he thought. "I'll get to see my children, spend the entire day with them, and I'll see them again on Sunday morning."

He was so happy, so grateful for having that chance for spending some time with his children, but he forgot who he was dealing with, and this morning, when he called Yu, she said, "You can't stay here with them. Visit later, stay for a couple of hours or so, but then go back to your place. Catch a cab home if you want."

M÷ sighed. Phone close to his left ear, he looked out of the window, took a deep breath, and saw that, unless he did something about it, Yu would always have control over him. Because the children lived with her she would always have a hold on M÷. Unless he did something about it.

"You know what? That's okay. I'll see them on Monday," M÷ said. It was Saturday. He hadn't seen his children since Thursday. That meant he would have to stay three days without seeing them. So be it. He was sick of having to run after Yu. A month ago, when she was having problems at their workplace (they work for the same company, in the same building, different departments, different hours; she works in the day, M÷ does the nightshift), she wanted M÷ at her place all the time, and she even spoke about them getting back together, remarry, buy a better place, but once her problems were sorted out, she went back to being her cruel self. Close call. Remarrying Yu would have been one of M÷'s biggest mistakes ever. Yes, close call, but the truth is the thought of remarrying Yu never crossed his mind.

Yu went silent. As for M÷, he had nothing else to say to her either. He was sick of being used, of being pushed around. A voice inside of him was telling him to, "Wait. Wait on the Lord. Wait on better days."

The world was still in lockdown.

The majority of people were still walking around with face masks on.

M÷'s landlady was still scared of the world, scared to leave her home.

As for M÷, he was tired of it all; tired of the propaganda, tired of the lies, tired of the media, the fake news, and, most of all, he was getting really tired and sick of Yu. He had spent more than a decade with her, 16 years or so of moaning and coldness.

Their marriage –and life together- had had some good moments, but, at times, Yu's coldness made the marriage insupportable. Whatever she said had to be the law or else!!!

As M÷ held the phone close to his ear he came to the conclusion that he wanted to live a life away from Yu, a life without her, and if he had to see less of his children for a while so be it. For now he would have to wait on better days, wait on the Lord, wait on a miracle, wait and hope, but he could no longer be running around Yu. The truth is she no longer deserved him.

Lamentations 3:26

M÷ would have to wait for a while, wait quietly, wait patiently, for better days to arrive. As for Yu, she could do as she pleased. And if she didn't want him at her place she was in her right to ask him to stay away. Or to tell him to visit as little as possible. But she couldn't expect him to go running back to her place whenever she had a problem and needed a shoulder to cry on.

She could no longer use him.

In fact, he was tired of being used.

It was time for him to take a break from it all, time to put his trust in the Lord.

Yes, it was time to wait.

Proverbs 3:5-6

...He shall direct your paths.

"Are you sure? You can visit. Or, if you want, I can drop the children at your place and get them later," Yu said. All of a sudden she didn't sound that confident. Or cold. Sometimes she kind of reminded him of Grandmother, and he was tired of women like that. Women who were always shouting at him, making fun of him, trying to bring him down and then make fun of his depression. It was better to be alone than to have women like that around him.

"No. Don't worry about it. I'll see you on Monday," he said. And that was that.

Yu had won. Or had she. Who knows?

Maybe there would be no winners. Only losers. And the children would be the losers. Then again, who knows?

The battle wasn't yet over and M÷ had righteousness on his side, but it would be a long battle where, at times, he would get so tired and down.

Once the call ended, M÷ felt kind of relieved. He could no longer, ever again, have Yu back in his life.

He got changed and went out.

"But go where? Where can I go?" he thought as he made his way down Tile Hill Lane.

The road in front of him looked so long, empty, cold. Without his children by his side, he felt empty, and he knew that the emptiness would be with him for a bit longer, too long, a lot longer than he expected, but he also had hope, a bit of hope, some faith, a bit of faith, and maybe that would be enough to keep him alive.

A couple walking on the opposite direction crossed the road when they saw M÷ just so they didn't have to walk past him. People avoided people. It was a cold age, an age of social distancing, face masks, countless lies in the media, countless lies everywhere. A cold age, an age of non-touching. If anything, that was the perfect world for cold-hearted Yu. But she would pay for everything she had done. And she would suffer too, just like M÷ was suffering. No one can outrun karma.

A few buses drove past him but M÷ didn't bother with them. Instead he walked all the way to Pool Meadow Bus Station where he then caught the bus 21 to Bell Green. He decided he would go and visit his friend Cassio in Riley Square. His friend was always telling him that he could visit whenever he wanted, and on that day M÷ decided to pay a visit to his friend and forget whatever was troubling him. Thinking about it wouldn't solve the problem. He needed a distraction, a change of thought. Needless to say his children were still on his mind. And he missed them so much but what could he do about it?

He needed distance (from Yu), some time on his own (time away from the Snake), time to reflect, time to write. Because of the divorce (and everything else in between) his writing and his dreams were suffering.

He needed to put Yu behind him once and for all and move on. His time would eventually come. His time with the children would come. His dreams would be achieved. He just needed to be patient. And he needed some distance from Yu.

Another close call?

Or another lie?

Asteroid 2001 FO32 will zoom past Earth on March 21 but NASA is saying that there's no need to worry.

In other news, Piers Morgan has left Good Morning Britain. *Will anyone actually miss him? Some of us probably will. After all, TV needs larger than life characters. Most of the people are so boring now, so WOKE, afraid of saying what's really on their minds. Not Piers. He says it out loud. No wonder some people like him. And no wonder some people hate him.*

March 6th, 202i (no typo error there; I've renamed 2021, turned it into a nameless year). When I got to Bell Green I didn't go straight away to Cassio's place. I couldn't.

When I found myself in Bell Green, I felt the need to have some time for myself so I just walked around the area, and then I sat down and felt the tears gather around the corners of my eyes.

I missed my children.

I missed what I had lost.

I missed what I never had.

I missed the parents that abandoned me when I was a child.

I missed the childhood that I could have but wasn't meant to happen.

I missed and I missed, but no one was missing me.

I sat near Farmfoods thinking what a failure I had been my entire life.

I had done nothing but mistake after mistake. To top it all, I married the wrong woman. But where was the right one?

Had I already lost her?

1999. A busy pub in Hammersmith. Achy has switched to Spanish but she's still telling me to go home with her and eat her pussy. Her exact words.

We're making our way to the front door, almost running towards the exit. Outside the pub, a couple are arguing. Achy stops on her tracks and says (to the couple, or to the man only), "Go home and eat her pussy."

Those words of Achy actually bring the argument to an end but now the couple are staring at Achy, and the last thing I want is to get into a fight.

I point at Achy and then make a smoking gesture with my fingers, followed by a drinking gesture. After that, nothing else happens and the couple go home.

"Damn! Maybe Achy is into something," I think.

I can't help laughing about it.

We kiss there, in the middle of the pavement, our lips and tongues tasting of cigarettes and alcohol. From there we head straight to Achy's place. The night is still young and there's something I must do for Achy. To Achy.

My mind relieves the past. What have I lost? But wasn't it meant to happen that way?

Cassio was really happy to see me at his place. My friend is retired, a bit poorly, and he has no family in England. As a matter of fact, he doesn't have a lot of family left anywhere, not even in Portugal, his country of birth.

We've been friends since 2008. We met at a Mormon church even though none of us is Mormon. I was there because of Yu, and Cassio had been invited to the service by a couple of Mormon missionaries'. The missionaries were trying to convert Cassio but he was (is) Catholic and Mormonism wasn't really his thing. Even though I'm not a Mormon, I've learned a few things throughout the years from that religion and I have met some good Mormon people.

Cassio made lunch for us. Fish, potatoes, vegetables, and Portuguese bread for lunch. I must say he's an excellent cook.

We ate and watched Portuguese telly. It had been a long time since I last watched Portuguese telly. Actually, I'm lying because, every once in a while (but rarely, if you want me to be honest), I watch a few Portuguese channels online.

After lunch, an espresso each.

Cassio's only companies are the birds that he keeps in a cage and the fishes in the aquarium. His English isn't that good (and he gets a bit nervous and shy when he has to speak the language) but he knows some Portuguese people in Coventry so he's never really alone. But, like me, he spends a lot of time on his own.

As I sat there with him, looking absentmindedly at the TV, looking but not really watching what was being shown, looking but not seeing, seeing but not really seeing, briefly, I forgot everything that was worrying me, but later, on the way back to Pool Meadow Bus Station, I started to miss my children, and I felt a bit depressed, lonely, and I didn't want to go back to my room in the middle of nowhere so I stayed in the city centre for a bit longer killing time. And later, much later, I got something to eat from a van in Broadgate. Some people that I vaguely know were there and we sat somewhere, on some footsteps that led into a building, on Hertford Street.

It was already dark, a few minutes to 8PM. I wanted to go home and do some writing but when I got home I went straight to bed.

I dreamt of the past, of a past love, of a life that seemed so far away, a life that could have been something else, a life with someone else.

1999. A warm room somewhere in London, the rain lashing against the window. A few minutes past 6AM and I'm already up, sitting on an old chair, reading Baudelaire, looking at a grey sky. Looking out of the window, I see someone running to the bus stop. An umbrella is running down the road, no one by its side. Achy is still sleeping, softly snoring. My notebook is waiting for me, waiting to be touched, waiting for some notes. I put the Baudelaire's book aside and I quickly go to the kitchen to get myself a cup of coffee. The other tenants are still sleeping. Maybe some of them have already left the house and went to work. I boil some water, pour some instant coffee into a mug, two spoons of sugar, and a few minutes later I'm back in the room. Achy is still sleeping. I swallow some coffee and then I write about last night. "Notes for nothing," I wonder. "Notes about nothing."

Writers like Fernando Pessoa, Henry Miller, and even Proust come to mind while I write. They're my inspiration, alongside life, alongside pain.

For the last few days I've been reading Sartre's *Nausea*. I finished reading that book two days ago and I started again from the beginning. And this morning, when I got up, I grabbed a book by Baudelaire and read some of his poetry. The book belongs to Achy. Like me, she's an avid reader but she has no writing ambitions. But what about me? What are my writing ambitions? For now, I wait on life to give me inspiration, and while I wait I write some notes about yesterday. And the day before. And…

March 8ᵗʰ, 2021. The kids are back at school. Well, some kids are.

I'm at Yu's place. I've just picked up our daughter Leaf from school. Our son Matthew only starts school next week. He's on Year 9. Leaf is on Year 3.

This afternoon Yu is in a better mood, smiling and everything, but it won't last. I saw her in the morning, briefly, from afar, when I was walking home, a few minutes before 8AM. She drove past me, and she saw me too. She was taking Leaf to school. It had been 3 days since I last had seen my daughter. I would have to wait a few more hours before I could see her and my son, and even then I would only be able to spend a few minutes with them.

A divorce can be hard on the children but it can be even harder on the parent that has to wait and wait for the time when he/she can finally see the children again.

Yu tells me I can spend the night at her place, even stay for the next few days. She's back at work tomorrow morning and I can stay at her place with our son Matthew, and later I can get Leaf from school and bring her back to Yu's place. Yu is smiling, telling me I can stay for a bit longer, but it's all a lie. We're living in the age of face masks and Yu always has a mask on. But that mask has fallen off because I can see her true (ugly) self. A person can be pretty on the outside but so ugly on the inside. Because she needs me this week, Yu is acting all nice towards me but it won't last. That's fine. For now, as I wait on better days to arrive, I swallow my pride and keep my true feelings hidden. My time will come. I just have to wait, patiently, for Life to give me more. But do I deserve better? More? I do.

I look at her face, the fake smile, a smile hidden behind an invisible mask. Years ago, she came running after me, chasing after me, going to London every month, almost begging me to marry her, not because she loved me but because she wanted to escape her parents. A few years down the road, she could no longer stand London so we moved to Coventry, into her parents' home. She's always running away from something, from someone, giving up on everything, on everyone.

She's building her own hole, a lonely hole. There's no place in there for me, thank G-d for it, but I'm fine with it because I don't want to be with her.

I want to smile.

I can't smile.

I can't look at her and smile.

I can't fake it.

"I can't stay. I have to catch the bus back to town in a few minutes," I say. Of course I want to stay and spend some time with my children, but I'm still upset. Upset, hurt and angry.

I shouldn't hold on to the anger.

I shouldn't let the hate consume me but I got tired of being used (and abused) by Yu, and now I don't want to spend a lot of time with her, close to her, in the same room as her, in the same house as her. I want distance from her, proper social distancing, miles and miles of distance. She made her own bed. It's a small bed and there's no place in there for me, and I'm okay with it.

I have a quick word with my son, then with my daughter; I kiss them both, and then I leave.

Of course, I'm sad.

Of course, I almost cry.

I'm only human.

I'm a father in pain, a father living away from his children, but, for now, I must wait. Better days will come.

2007 to 2020 (even 2021, but it's over now): I cook, hoover, work, tidy up around the home, iron the clothes, and do so much more, but nothing is ever good enough for Yu. What does she want from me? She wants everything without ever giving a thing back.

I've been going for long walks ever since the first lockdown started in March 2020. The moment they said, "Stay home," I went out.

I went everywhere, met hundreds of people, spent time alone, in the dark, in the woods, praying, crying.

In my defence, by then my marriage was already coming to an end, and to forget everything I went for long walks.

I always made sure to take a book with me, sometimes even a bottle of water just in case I got thirsty.

I read Bolaño, Patti Smith, Fernando Sdrigotti, Gao Xingjian, Ma Jian, biographies, Kabbalistic books, and I wrote two novels, both about the virus. Or about a virus. And while I was patrolling the city, going through my own Dark Night of the Soul, dying but not dying, Yu was building a new life for herself behind my back, a life of fake smiles and a few lies, a life where she was the heroine of a fairy tale, a princess when she failed to realise that she was a witch, not a princess, a witch and a snake, not a princess or a fairy.

Who knows what kind of lies she told about me to her religious friends? But do I care about it? I don't, and sooner or later the lies will catch up with her.

Yu is going against Nature. She's putting a dare on Karma, spitting on Life, stepping on Love, not realising that one day she will have to pay for what she's doing. Loneliness is waiting on her, waiting patiently because loneliness is very patient.

I made long walks in the dark during those troubled times, literally in the dark because I went out at night and walked for hours without a destination, and at certain times my eyes got a bit blurry because I found myself crying even while walking, but even the tears didn't stop me from walking. Metaphorically speaking, it was a long walk in the dark because there were times when I went out early in the morning for a long walk, but the darkness was there, inside of me, always present, a darkness that told me to quit and end it all, a darkness inside me, eating me away, some sort of spiritual depression, and it went on for a long time, that existential crisis, that illusion I had about life, but bit by bit I started to open my eyes and to see beyond the darkness, see past the Dark Night of the Soul, see that all the illusions I had about what really matters were lies and that I didn't have to impress anyone, and once I was free, free from the lies and the darkness, I started to see a lot of people that I know for what they really are (and I didn't like what I was seeing) (and I also saw that a lot of them didn't care for anyone but themselves) (and I saw so much selfishness and dark souls) (and I saw that the world was an ugly place, or parts of it were, and that the ones who control everything were creating division and chaos amongst the people so that we couldn't see how strong and beautiful we are, but we're only strong and beautiful if we stay united) (and I also saw that there isn't such things as race or colour; we're one: we're the human race, a family of different beings, but our greedy rulers don't want us to know that), and I saw that a lot of people that I love were jealous of my happiness, so jealous of the little that I had, and their jealousy was so strong, scarily strong, stronger than love. And I also saw that Yu is nothing but a snake. A poisonous viper. A venomous ungrateful rattlesnake. A tiger snake, highly venomous. Throughout the years she did nothing but complain, and nothing I did was ever good enough for her. I bought her expensive coats, took her out to dinner various times, bought her clothes, food, a camcorder, watch, shoes, etc., etc., so much shit for that poisonous snake, but nothing was ever good and she always complained. And when it came to her buying a present for anyone, she always bought the cheapest stuff she could find. Yu wants it all but she doesn't want to give a thing back. That's not how the world works. That's not how life works. Life gives but you must give back.

I went for long walks, blurry walks, lonely walks, sad walks, walks where I spoke to the sky, and I asked, "Lord, why am I losing everything again? My parents left me when I was a child and now You're taking my children away from me. Why?

"Please, Lord, don't do this to me. Don't take my children away from me."

Day after day, I made the long walk to work, always leaving home a bit early so that I could stop somewhere and cry. And I also cried at home, locked in what used to be mine and Yu's bedroom (but by then she was sleeping in the kids bedroom, sleeping without a care in the world, the careless snake, sleeping long hours, snoring loudly while I hardly slept) or in the bathroom.

I cried for what I had lost and for what I was about to lose.

Yu knew that I was crying but she didn't give a damn. But that's okay.

The world turns dark and we must get used to the darkness, if only temporarily, but one day someone removes the blind from our eyes and a bright path appears in front of us. The darkness will then be replaced by brightness, but we must never forget the darkness or the friends who stood by our side when we were feeling our way in the dark.

Yu put a hood over my head before pushing me into the darkness. And then she laughed. Right now, she's still laughing; laughing when she gets home from work and sits her fat ass on her new sofa, a sofa that was probably bought with my money, laughing when she goes to visit her religious friends and eats their food and spends time with them while I'm alone, laughing because she has everything and I have nothing, but she shouldn't laugh so much. Too much laughter is bad for a person's health.

Even one of my brothers is jealous of me, jealous of the fact I have nothing. I don't understand people.

To forget everything that was troubling me (but I still remember all, and I even wrote about it, lest I forget it), I went for long walks, and one time, when I was sitting at a park in Broomfield Place, I saw a man reading Viktor Shklovsky's *Third Factory*, and that man also looked troubled. I sat there reading something by Nikolai Leskov while occasionally I would look at the other man. And then I wrote in my journal while the other man lit a cigarette. The park was almost empty. Minutes later, two other men appeared and sat on the grass. One of them lit a joint, and then they started to badmouth someone else. And then the park got quite busy, with people walking their dogs or coming out for a walk and a smoke. I guess people were tired of staying at home. Two women were sitting on the grass, sharing a big bottle of Coke and eating crisps. A man and a woman were walking their dog. Two men were sitting on a bench, smoking and talking. I realised that they were the ones who only a few minutes ago had sat on the grass to share a joint. Another man, sitting on the grass, was browsing through his phone.

The man reading Shklovsky got up and made his way out of the park. A few minutes later, I too stood up and went for a walk, only to bump into the Shklovsky reader by Upper Spon Street. He was sitting on a wall, waiting. There were others there with him, waiting, just waiting.

I saw then that they were waiting to be fed because they were sitting outside a food bank. I joined them and sat there, next to the Shklovsky reader, and waited to be fed too. Little did I know then that that action of mine would lead me to meet hundreds of new faces throughout the year. And later, I too would help out on a food bank. And I would meet more people, some of which would become sort of friends with me. Life gave me something, I gave something back, and then Life gave me more. That's how the world works.

The walks went on. Long walks. Sad walks. Thoughtful walks. Tearful walks.

I saw a woman sitting on a bench by Ironmonger Row reading Paul B. Preciado's *An Apartment On Uranus*. I wrote the name of that book down. Then I went inside Greggs and got myself a Yum Yum and a hot chocolate. The body was hungry. The body was tired. And my right knee was aching. But I couldn't stop.

I left Greggs and saw that the Preciado reader was still sitting outside, still reading Preciado and smoking a cigarette. She was a young woman, early twenties, peroxide-blond, dark eye lashes, pale skin, long legs, thin. I crossed the road, walked past Primark, and saw a young man sitting on a bench outside the banks on Broadgate, a Starbucks cup next to him. The young man was reading Shen Fu's *Six Records of a Floating Life*; I actually misspelled it when I wrote the title down, calling it *Six Records of a Gloating Life*. A few meters ahead, I caught sight of another man glued to a book. He was reading Charles Simic.

"Has everyone suddenly found a love of literature? Is the lockdown and the virus –the Invisible Enemy- pushing people towards literature?" I thought.

I kept on walking, finished my Yum Yum and my hot chocolate, and made my way home, a home that soon wouldn't be my home, a home that felt like a prison. When I got home, I saw that Yu was already in bed, resting her fat arse. She was laughing while watching something on her phone. She had reasons to laugh, after all, soon she would be moving into her new place, she had a job, which I got her, and she was being paid to stay at home and do nothing. What more could she want? Oh, knowing Yu as I know her now, she wanted a lot more.

The children were still in the living room, playing Roblox. I changed into my pyjamas, brushed my teeth, said my prayers, told the children to turn their computers off, and then the three of us went to bed. We slept in the big bed, a bed that used to be mine and Yu's, a bed where I was never really loved.

Yu was still laughing. She had reasons to laugh.

Writers

2021, March 13th. Another day without seeing my children. And I probably won't see them tomorrow either. How ironic. Maybe sad is the right word. But I say ironic because I booked this Saturday and last Saturday as holidays because I wanted to spend some time with my children, but, in the end, my plans went down the drain. New plans were then made. It was either that or stay at home, alone with the darkness; that enemy known as depression. So, as I've already mentioned (a case of repetition here; nothing new with that when it comes to my writing), new plans were made, and both last Saturday and today, I've decided to visit my friend Cassio in Bell Green, have lunch at his place (and Cassio is such a good cook – and a good friend), watch a bit of Portuguese telly even though I can't stand TV, but it's better than being alone, stuck in my bedroom, alone with the sadness (or you call it darkness, even depression). Then again, I could have just stayed in my bedroom and write, read a few chapters of the Bible, rest, sleep, meditate, but Cassio also needs company, and he's a good friend, such a good friend, although slightly crazy, a friend who was there when I most needed one (and I can't forget that even though, as I've already mentioned, he's slightly crazy), so I did the right thing and went to visit my friend. Then again, I could have just stayed in my bedroom and write (and I did have some writing to do but it would have to wait).

The other two people in the house where I live were still in their bedrooms. One of them, the landlady, whose room faces mine, was in bed, sleeping. She always goes to bed really late. The one downstairs, a young Christian woman, was already up; I could hear her laughing, but she was still in her bedroom. I went downstairs, showered, ate breakfast, got changed, and left the house. A few minutes later I was inside the 6A bus, heading towards the city centre. I was the only passenger who wasn't wearing a face mask. Before you go bananas and jump on the keyboard to attack me, I've got a heart problem, and the constant use of a face mask gives me breathing problems and that's why I stopped using one.)

Once in town, I went to a Portuguese minimarket called Gorety, situated by the Coventry Canal Basin. It was a windy day and later it would rain. **Yu was probably at...** I cleared my mind of negative thoughts as I made my way up the road. Two young women walked past me, no masks on as they made their way down the road. I heard them talking. They were Portuguese. I gave them a quick glance. They were both pretty, both too young for me. As I watched them make their way down the road, I wondered when I would love again.

I resumed my walk, saw a Tesco worker leaning against the wall, smoking and talking on the phone, he was a young man, mid-thirties, blond, thin hair. He didn't even glance my way when I walked past him.

I climbed the steps, walked over the bridge, saw a man making his way towards me, an angry look on his face, a face mask covering a bit of his anger, but his eyes, and even his forehead, couldn't disguise his anger. He was older than me, in his sixties I would say, maybe older than that. He walked past me and grunted. Yu too has mastered the art of grunting.

I got a few bits from Gorety, including some *cevada* (barley) from Portugal, and then made my way to Pool Meadow Bus Station.

I caught the 21 bus heading towards Bell Green.

I sat almost at the back, behind a man who was reading Dostoevsky. He was a bit older than me, or at least he looked to be older than me, and he was wearing a long black coat, same as me. A long black coat over a bright blue T-shirt. He was reading *House of the Dead*, a book I've read many years ago. As for me, I had a book by Imre Kertész with me, but I wasn't reading. I was too busy watching others around me, the people inside the bus and even life outside the bus.

The bus drove past a lot of small shops, butchers selling halal meat, minimarkets with lots of food outside, a few takeaway shops, and it took me a while to realise that the Dostoevsky reader was also a writer. He had put the book down, to his left (or should I say on the left seat?), and he was writing something in a notebook. Since I was sitting behind him, I managed to read some of his notes (but I won't write them here; it wouldn't be fair, after all, it's his own life, maybe his own book, a book that might never be published, maybe another *Book of Disquiet*, a quiet masterpiece, but, nevertheless, it's still his book, his story to tell), and from what I read, I could tell that he was writing some sort of journal. I leaned back and sat straight, diverting my eyes from what he was writing, and I gave the writer a better look. Like I've mentioned before, he wore a long black coat, a blue T-shirt, jeans, and a pair of Adidas trainers. He looked to be somewhere between 40 to mid-fifties. He had a young face but whatever hair he had left was totally white, thin up front, already going bald. A bit of a stubble, and even his stubble was completely white. He was still writing when I got out of the bus, and watching him write made me want to sit somewhere and write too, but my friend Cassio was waiting for me so the writing would have to be put on hold. But I still sat downstairs, although briefly, by the bus stop, where I quickly wrote down some notes lest I forget some of the events.

The area outside Cassio's building was quite busy, especially Farmfoods and the Polish supermarket next to it. Even Nisa was busy. Cassio had everything he needed nearby. Later, when I was in his apartment, I even said, "You don't need to go anywhere. You've got everything you need just outside your building, even a library."

Cassio nodded.

At Cassio's place we spoke about literature, especially Portuguese literature, and about (Portuguese) writers and poets that Cassio likes, people like Teixeira de Pascoas, a poet I've never read, Aquilino Ribeiro, Camilo Castelo Branco, Luís Miguel Rocha, Alexandre Herculano, Florbela Espanca, and, of course, our favourite, the disquiet author, the great Fernando Pessoa. And then we spoke about Kenzaburo Oe, a writer that Cassio has never read and who happens to be one of my favourite authors, and I told myself that I would try and find a Portuguese translation of one of Oe-san's works so that Cassio could read this wonderful writer.

After lunch, I sat down on Cassio's sofa and dozed off for an hour or so. I sure needed the rest.

Cassio is also a writer. A minimalistic writer. A lazy writer. A tired writer. A sick writer.

Due to his bad health (and bad eye sight; he's actually blind in one eye, or almost blind), Cassio can't write for a long period of time, plus, when it comes to writing, he's lazy, undedicated, unwilling to give more to it.

He has a couple of typewriters at home, both still working, and he has some notes written down, and loose papers lying around, all over his apartment, and his story is one that deserves to be told, but Cassio doesn't has the disciple needed to become an author, which is a shame because his story is really good. But, again, it's not up to me to write it. And I only know a few details, not the whole plot.

Sylvia wants to have sex. Those are her exact words when she messages me: "I want to have sex." The sentence is followed by a thoughtful emoji.

Is that an invitation?

I hope not.

Does she want to have sex with me?

I hope not.

I don't know what to write back.

I'm in my bedroom listening to Erik Jackson's *Long After Midnight*. A boring Sunday morning. The sun is out, a few minutes after 8AM, and I'm already up, glued to the laptop. Soon I will shower, and then head to the church in Fleet Street. The service lasts for around one hour. Once the service is over I might waste a couple of hours in town, sit somewhere and finish the book by Kertész.

Sylvia is also up, probably writing nothing in her almost empty notebook. She wants to write a novel. At least that's what she told me five years ago. Five years later, still nothing, nothing but a blank page.

I read her message, again and again, and I don't know what to say.

In the end I say nothing.

Sylvia says nothing either.

I don't want sex.

I want love.

A lot of people are saying no the vaccines against the Invisible Enemy. I said no long time ago. My friend Leo took the first vaccine last Saturday, March 13th. I met up with him on Sunday, March 14th, and Leo told me that he felt like crap. And he sure looked it. The area around his eyes was really pale, kind of yellowish, which is a bit of a worry. Or maybe not. Maybe it's only the side-effects of the vaccine and later he will go back to normal.

Leo is a strong black man, born in England but his parents are from Jamaica. He used to be a bouncer and an amateur boxer. From what he told me ages ago, when he was a young man he got himself into a lot of fights. He was an angry young man; that's what he told me, but now he's calmed down. Well, sort of. He's still a bit loud, a bit of a joker, a cool character, and I really like him.

We became friends last year, at St. Paul's Church in Foleshill Road, and every Sunday we meet up by Pool Meadow Bus Station. I help out at a food bank facility where we hand out food to the needy. Leo comes there for food. I also take some food home with me. Not much. Just enough for a couple of days.

After the food is given out, I grab myself some hot food, a cup of soup and a cup of coffee, and I stand close to Leo and some other people, eating and talking. I've been doing this for quite a while now, and helping out at the food bank has helped me out as well.

Empty your mind of all thoughts.

Become nobody, nothing, be nowhere.

The outer world isn't real.

Empty your mind of all distractions, meet your consciousness halfway, be one with it, and design your life.

The unknown is waiting for you.

Discover it.

Embrace it.

Become who you want to be.

March 16ᵗʰ. A cold windy afternoon.

A few hours' sleep out of the way, I got up, showered, got changed, and went to Coventry market for lunch. Luckily I didn't miss the bus. And I didn't have to wait too long for it. Seconds after I had arrived at the bus stop, I turned around and saw the 6A bus slowly making its way towards me. I lifted my hand in the air, a futile gesture since the bus driver was already signalling to the traffic behind him that he was going to stop.

I entered the bus, sat right at the front, on one of the seats "designed" for disabled people or people with pushchairs, looked to my right and saw an older woman reading Gene Wolfe. I know who Gene Wolfe is but I've never read any of his sci-fi novels. I wrote his name down, in one of my notebooks. My children were on my mind, in my thoughts, but thinking about them made me sad. I focused my thoughts on nothing (and on everything). The world would have to wait. This world…

Briefly, Yu visited my thoughts. I saw her sitting her fat arse on her new sofa, Netflix on, a couple of bags of crisps on her lap, and… And I cleared my mind, emptied it of all thoughts.

I saw a long road ahead, an "invisible" road, a road that was both real and unreal, a road that was waiting for me, a path that I would have to travel on my own, but that doesn't necessarily meant that I would be alone. Is just that certain journeys you have to make it alone, leave those who no longer matter behind (because they're holding you back) (because they emit bad energy, and their bad energy stops your progress) (because they no longer matter and all that doesn't matter must be forgotten), and you must travel alone, alone with your conscience and you "Other Self", the Being Within, the light that connects you to the Watcher; He who is able to do Everything, and that shows you that even though you're travelling on your own, you're not necessarily alone.

I was so lost in the nothingness of my thoughts I almost missed my stop.

The wind was blowing softly. I felt the cold on my cheeks, smiled, crossed the road, and noticed that the city centre was starting to get busier. People were sick of being at home, sick of the lockdown, sick of the lies, sick of the media, sick because of the Invisible Enemy, sick because of depression, sick because they couldn't go to the doctor and get a check-up. The world was dying, committing the longest suicide of all, being killed by the Invisible Hand. Who could save us? Jordan Petterson? No, of course not. But he too was becoming a believer, turning to Christus. There was still hope but…

Even Christ was being cancelled by some people, being called out by the Woke Generation.

There was still hope but the enemy was growing, growing because of the lie that was being fed. It wasn't my fight, or so I thought, but unless I was willing to give up my freedom it was my fight. But how can you fight the Invisible Hand that rules over all?

I grabbed a chicken roll and a cup of coffee from a market stall, total £2.60, cheaper than a cup of coffee at Starbucks, and then I sat outside, on a small wall facing the market.

The mind was blank. Free of bad energy.

I smiled and enjoyed my food.

Soon I would be seeing my children, then I would go to work. For now, life is giving me everything I need. I want more but now, for some reason that is unknown to me, it's not the right time for more. More will come. I just need to wait.

The Being Within was talking to me, in the present, telling me to slow down and listen. Because of life, and because of erratic thoughts, or should I say because of confusion, the confusion/chaos within me, the confusion-chaos that comes with the troubles of life, my mind was all over the place when the right thing was to slow down, think of nothing, and listen. Listen to the Within, the Other Self, the One who sees it all. Listen and wait: nothing good comes out of rushing.

Thursday, March 18th. Laundry day. A cold day, too.

A long never-ending white cloud seems to have taken over the whole city.

M÷ spent the night at his ex-wife's place and in the morning he took the 6A bus back to his place. Once home, he grabbed his laundry bag, then took the 10 bus that stopped by the Albany pub, only a minute's walk from the laundrette. Before he left her place, Yu asked him if he wanted a lift home but he said no. He was still upset.

He who can Forgive All wanted for M÷ to forgive Yu (because He Who Forgives All would deal with her later on, much later, so there was no reason for M÷ to be upset) so that he could be forgiven too (and M÷'s name was also written in the Book of Life), but M÷ couldn't forgive her. Not yet.

Last night, at her place, she was back to being her cruel self, back to mocking M÷, and while she mocked him she laughed, and not only was she laughing, she was also being snobby and arrogant. And bossy. Actually, bitchy would be a better word to describe her.

Because she was at home, and the children were living with her; in a way, they were hers (and M÷ was only a part-time dad), Yu thought she could treat M÷ like crap and get away with it. After all, if he said anything she didn't like, she could always tell him not to return to her place, which she did before, and then M÷ wouldn't be able to see much of his children. And that happened before too.

A few times during the night, she shushed him and told him to be quiet, and she addressed him as one would address a dog, as a cruel owner would address a dog. M÷ took a deep breath and tried so hard not to lose his temper. Seeing that Yu brought out the worst in him that was a hard task to accomplish. Nonetheless, he told her not to speak to him like that. After all, he wasn't her dog.

Okay, she had the kids.

Okay, she had a bit of power over him, or so she thought, but the truth was he was clearing out his mind, emptying it of her, and if she wanted to take the children away from him, so be it. In the end, Nature would get her; Karma would give her a big kick in the ass, and if M÷ had to be without the children for a while so be it.

The children were important to him but so was his mind. And his mind could no longer deal with Yu's cruelty. She was digging a hole for herself, pushing M÷ further and further away from her life, and she thought she was the One, better than everyone else, and that she would never need anyone else because she was Magnificent, or so she thought, but the truth was she was living a lie, a lie created by her pathetic little brain. Maybe she was going through the worst menopause in the history of the world

"I don't care if this is your house or not, but don't shush me," M÷ said, keeping his cool when he addressed the snake sitting next to him.

He almost went home but then he found himself in the other bedroom with his son Matthew. And Matthew was crying, crying because he knew his father no longer wanted to be there, never again, crying because he knew his father wanted to leave, leave not only that place but also that city, leave for good, and Matthew knew his father wanted to disappear (M÷ told him so, repeatedly, not last night but previously); move somewhere else, really far away, and start a new life, and Matthew feared losing his father even though M÷ told him repeatedly, not last night but previously, that he would always be there for Matthew, and that they would always have to stay in touch. Of course, M÷ wasn't going anywhere. Not then. Not yet.

Not so long ago, a rabbi friend of his gave him a chance to start a new life, a life in another city, a life that he so badly needed, but how could he leave his children behind?

M÷ knew too well how it was to live a life without his parents nearby and he didn't want that life for his children. But then one day Matthew and Leaf would move away, start their own lives. What would be of M÷ then?

Laundry out of the way, M÷ takes the 10 bus to Pool Meadow Bus Station. He has to renew his monthly bus pass, and afterwards he'll get another chicken roll and a cup of coffee from the market. That's lunch out of the way.

Afterwards?

Afterwards, home. Back to the bedroom that is now his home.

Less than one hours' rest and he's up, gets changed, and gets the 10 bus that will take him to his daughter's school.

Not much of a life, but he can't complain either. It could be worse and he knows it.

I write to remember what was done and said to me when I was at my lowest. Later on, when my life is better, the same people that ignored me when I most needed them might try to fool me with soft words and fake smiles, but I've got it all written down, in my own book of life;

their actions and lies, and it will take more than soft words and fake smiles to fool me again.

You cannot see G-D without holiness.

Holiness is a shield.

Be holy. Protect yourself.

Others may try to hurt you but if you're holy G-D's with you.

If you are indeed a child of G-D, prove it by being holy with a holy life.

No holiness, no heaven.

Psalm 116:1-2

You cannot see G-D without holiness.

Psalm 67:1

But sometimes it is hard to be holy all the time.

Sometimes it is hard to forgive those who have hurt you so much.

Sometimes, because of hate, it is hard to see holiness.

March 18th. After getting his daughter from school, they take the 6A bus back to Yu's place. Leaf hugs her dad and doesn't let go of him during the entire journey. They always enjoy those moments together. For now, it's the best (the most) they can get.

Yu is at home a few minutes after 5PM. This afternoon she's in a better mood but her mood can change in a matter of seconds. Nowadays M÷ finds her tiring and boring, not to mention fake as a snake, devious, and he can't imagine how he managed to marry a woman like that. But now it's too late and because they have children together, he will have to remain in touch with her for quite a long time. But sooner or later the Universe will switch and reverse or whatever, and M÷ will get his rewards while Yu will get what she deserves. He takes a deep breath and waits… He waits on the Universe to watch his back, on G-D to stop him from falling (into darkness, temptation, sadness), and at times, while he waits, he feels a bit of anger inside him, anger put in there by Yu's actions, but he must let go of that anger.

The children are playing on their laptops. Leaf is playing Roblox while Matthew is playing Steam. And Yu is being so nice towards M÷, telling him that he can visit anytime and stay whenever he wants. Only yesterday she was telling him she doesn't want for him to visit that much, stay for too long, and she acted so cold towards him, and even mocked him when she saw the sadness in his eyes (but today she's seeing the anger, the indifference, maybe even hate), and today she's being so nice towards him. Maybe she has noticed that he's being indifferent to her, going cold too, but only towards her. She pushed him and pushed him and pushed him (and abused him and made fun of him and called him fat and stupid), and when he was at his lowest, on the brink of dying, she laughed her head off, but now, slowly, he's lifting himself up, and, in the process, he's forgetting her (but not forgiving her, not yet). Maybe, finally, Yu has seen that he no longer cares about her. The Yu he used to love has died, a spiritual death, and she no longer lives in his memory. Instead, she was replaced by a devious snake. And maybe now she's afraid; deep inside, she's afraid of the loneliness that will one day arrive, an almost self-imposed loneliness, and she's finally realising that M÷ won't always be there for her. Unknown to her, he's already planning a new life, a life where he will have as little contact as he can with her, a life free of Yu.

He wants to live a quiet life, a life of prayer and silence, a life where he can dedicated himself to the Lord.

He wants (and needs) a new home, a proper home, a small place where he can be at ease, a place of prayer, a home of rest, a place where he can grow some food and where his children can be with him. He's working for that place; for his home and for a life of simplicity and harmony, a private life, a life shared only with those he loves.

He looks at his watch. Ten minutes before the next bus arrives. He kisses his children goodbye and exits the living room. That's not his home. That will never be his home. Not so long ago, knowing that saddened him. Now he's happy that he no longer has to share a home with Yu.

As always, Matthew looks really sad to see his father leaving.

Yu comes to the door and says, "See you, pappy."

When they were married she used to call him pappy all the time, or most of the time, but then she went cold, really cold, stone cold, as cold as marble, as cold as death; colder even, and she used to grunt and hiss at him, and when she finally went back to work she screamed, "I WANT YOU OUT OF THIS HOUSE!!!!", day after day, "I WANT YOU OUT OF THIS HOUSE!!!", but then she lost her job, came running back to his arms, literally running, almost crying, and said, "Pappy, I'm going to lose my job."

She sounded so weak and fragile, so different from her now-cold self, and he, the poor fool, the ever-forgiving romantic (but that was yesterday, so long ago, before he died inside, and nowadays he's no longer the ever-forgiving romantic), said, "Don't worry about it. I'm working. I can look after the four of us. After all, I've been doing that for more than ten years now."

For more than ten years, they survived mainly on his wages, and she even managed to save some money. Since he was a fool in love (and maybe that will save him in the World to Come), he always made sure that Yu always put some money aside for herself. The poor fool (in love) thought that they would always stay together.

After losing her job, Yu went quiet, and she even became a bit nicer towards him. Shortly afterwards she found another job, but then she quit that job. And afterwards she found another job. She quit that one too. From what she told M÷, everyone was against her. She was a heroine fighting a horde of villains, and the villains could be found on every job she went to. M÷ didn't know what to say or do about it. Yu couldn't just quit every single job. That would look bad on her resume. Unknowingly to him, she was also planning to quit on him, but, being unemployed, she needed him, and the poor fool, what a fool, foolish clown, kept on working, and later he even found her a job at his workplace. That was heaven sent to her. The moment she got the job she started to plan a life without M÷. He had served his purpose. Now it was time to get rid of him.

She planned it all carefully, every little detail, checked and rechecked. Then came the Invisible Enemy, the virus that stopped the world, the lockdown, but virus or no virus, lockdown or no lockdown, Yu wanted a new life without M÷. Meanwhile the poor fool kept on working for the family, always being the devoted father and husband, what a fool, what a clown, sad clown, pathetic faithful fool, and he bought loads of foods, just in case, for the entire family, and while he spent most of his wages on the family, greedy Yu saved every penny. After all, she had a plan, and her plan didn't include M÷ the clown, sad clown, pathetic faithful fool.

Psalm 37:7

And when M÷ lost everything, he almost went crazy, and he asked the Lord, "Why?" but he got no reply.

Psalm 37:8

She took everything, even the children, and then she laughed while he was crying.

Friday 19ᵗʰ. Yu's speech has gone soft but I know better than to trust her. She can lose her temper in a matter of seconds, go back to her cold self, so, when I'm around her, I never let my guard down. In a way, our roles have slightly been reversed now; I'm the one who has gone cold now but this coldness (indifference) of mine is a shield, some kind of protection against the lies and the liars that surround me. Even at work I'm surrounded by lies and liars.

Yu says, "You can come here tomorrow."

A soft speech, almost sweet. A lie? Only she knows. Then again, maybe not even she knows it.

A cat is rolling around Yu's back garden. I always wanted to have a house with my own back garden, a small place where I could grow my own vegetables. One day, maybe. Soon, maybe.

"I can't. I already have plans," I say, which is true.

Tomorrow I'm going to Cassio's place for lunch. When I was at my lowest Cassio was there for me, and he even offered me a place to sleep in case I needed it. That's a true friend; a rare thing nowadays.

I kiss my children goodbye. I'll see them again in a few days' time, maybe on Monday. Matthew opens the front door for me and gives me a big hug. He's so tall now. He's growing so fast and I'm missing it all.

Life goes by so fast and, before you know it, those you love have grown and left home. Enjoy every minute you can with them.

My mother isn't too well. She's on a fight against cancer, battling hard. I wish I could spend more time with Mother. Even that was taken away from me.

Mother's a fighter, a warrior. She never complains.

She's not too happy with Yu and she told me so. And then she told me to tell it to Yu but I couldn't be bothered. And what would have been the point of it? It would only lead to another pointless, unwanted argument with Yu and I've already had too many of those throughout the years. Now I want a life without Yu. It will come, soon, I hope.

March 20th. Yu texted me, asked me if I could go to her place after work and look after the children. I can sleep, shower, and even have lunch there, and then she'll cook dinner for me to take to work, she said. On Sundays she tends to go to a friend's house for some sort of religious service, and the children go with her, but Leaf doesn't want to go; she's insisting that she's not going and she wants to see me so Yu asked if I could stay with them.

"Of course," I say to myself.

"Of course," I reply.

The Being Within has told me to wait, not to rush things and stop chasing after other people.

"Let them chase you," the Voice Within said.

What does it know that I don't?

Everything...

March 21st. After work I go to McDonald's on 26 Cross Cheaping for breakfast. Then I sit outside, eating and drinking. Some people are already out, waiting for a bus that will take them to work or home. A few customers inside McDonald's. A few at Starbucks too. A pigeon is eating a Snickers chocolate bar on the road, close to the pavement.

Two other pigeons walk on by, past us, but neither of them stops for a snack. Maybe they don't like chocolate.

I finish my breakfast and make my way to Pool Meadow Bus Station.

I'm alone, one with the world, alone with my thoughts, one with G-D.

There are times when impure thoughts try to take over my mind but I (try to) banish them away with short prayers. As a child I was taught bad things, saw dirty images, and for a long time I tried in vain to banish bad thoughts and dirty images from my mind, and only last year, after I lost everything (and nothing), after I almost went mad, after I made my way blindly through the Dark Night of the Soul, did I finally managed to leave the dirty images behind me. I'll be honest here and admit that there were a couple of relapses along the way, short relapses, brief relapses (but they happened so I'm guilty), but I was strong enough to leave it all behind, and instead of having impure thoughts and watching dirty images, I retreated into a corner of my soul, my happy place, a place I go to by meditating.

Last year, something (maybe someone) inside of me died, or left for good, and I no longer want that person or thing inside of me.

I wait inside the station for thirty minutes for the 6A bus to arrive. I read a few pages of Ben Lerner's *The Topeka School*. There's only one person close to me and he seems to be sleeping. I wonder if he has missed his bus. A pretty woman is standing outside, smoking. She keeps looking my way and I keep looking at her. Starved lovers, I wonder.

The world is changing, becoming darker, colder, turning into a bad sci-fi novel. Moloch is here, or at least it looks like it. In fact, right now I feel as if I'm a character in the *Book of Revelation*, just waiting for the Mark and the End to arrive. But the End isn't actually the End. The End (in *Book of Revelation*) is actually a new beginning. It is, isn't it? Maybe I need to read it again.

After my breakup, months down the road, I went back to Christ, but I've already mentioned this, haven't I? While my breakup was happening, I was losing my faith, even the will to live, but once I moved out, I felt the need for Christ in my life, and so I changed my way of being, my way of thinking, even my way of living. Because of meditation, I was already changing, slowly changing, but the breakup was the push that I needed for a complete change.

The bus finally arrives. I'm its only passenger but a stop later someone else gets in the bus. Later, when the bus is already close to Bannerbrook Park, and I'm its only passenger, a dreamer travelling through a nightmare or through a deserted landscape where nothing seems to happen, a landscape long time ago inhabited by dreamers and lost poets, the bus stops to let in two passengers. I watch as two men in their sixties enter the bus, both of them wearing face masks. They make their way to the back of the bus, and the second man is wearing not only a face mask but also plastic gloves, like the ones surgeons and nurses wear. He slows his pace when he sees me, and he looks me up and down. He's probably wondering why I'm not wearing a face mask.

He gives me a long look. Actually, he gives me daggers and then moves along.

The time might come when those who refuse to take the vaccine(s) and don't wear face masks will be persecuted, not only by the media and the government but also by the people. Past mistakes will quickly be forgotten as humankind, or parts of it, become some sort of demons. It will happen soon, I believe; I've already warned some friends of it. I'm ready for it. And I'm not. Mentally, I'm ready for the worse, waiting for it, but I also fear it. Hopefully I'm wrong and it will never come.

For some reason (and she won't tell us why), Leaf doesn't want to go to the religious service at the house of Yu's friend. Something happened there, in that house, but Leaf won't say what. Instead of trying to force it out, I decide to wait and give her some time. I know how my daughter thinks. She doesn't like it when people try to pressure her into doing or saying something so I'll wait, and I'll give her some time, and later, probably tomorrow, after school, I'll ask her again what happened.

"Sometimes I like to read novels without plot, novels where you just follow the narrator through a long journey," I say.

Sima nods.

We're sitting on the steps of Holy Trinity Church, drinking overpriced coffee from paper cups. Sima paid for the drinks so I shouldn't be complaining.

"Like Proust..." she says, then a long pause follows. "Have you ever read Proust?"

"Of course. He's one of my favourite authors," I say.

"Really?"

"Yes."

Two pigeons are walking back and forth, looking at us, hoping, waiting. They want food but neither Sima nor I have anything to give to them.

A couple of construction workers sit a few meters away from us, on a wall, eating their lunch. People walking up and down the street, getting into buses, drinking from Starbucks paper cups, listening to music on their phones. Sima has an iPhone but it's a cheap one. She's not into the latest gadget and doesn't feel the need to show off.

She's a Christian, born again, a follower of Christ.

She told me once that she almost lost it all because of depression, but then, in Christ, she found a reason to live.

We met last year, outside this same church, and we became friends.

"I like Sebald," she says.

"I love Sebald," I say.

I mention a novel to her, written by Teju Cole, a novel (and a writer) that reminds me of Sebald. Then she tells me about a novel by Péter Nádas called *A Book of Memories*, and I tell her that I have that book but still haven't read it. And then she tells me about a novel by Marcel Möring called *In Babylon*, and I tell her that I also have that book but still haven't read it.

Sima gives me a long look and I laugh about it.

"Don't look at me like that. I do have those books but I've been reading other writers, writers like André Breton, André Gide, and Poe, whom I've never read until a few months ago," I said.

The truth is I have a lot of books that I bought ages ago still waiting to be read, so many that I've decided not to buy any new books for a long time.

We were still taking about books when we saw a couple of police officers on the distant horizon, making their way toward us. Maybe there weren't heading our way, and I have nothing against police officers; I know how hard their work must be and how much abuse they put up with, but we're living in very strange times, times where (sigh) at times the police pursue the innocent. We're living at a time when people are told to stay apart, keep the distance, fight the depression on your own, alone, don't love, stay home, obey the coldness (meanwhile, our leaders are having affairs), and when Sima and I saw the police officers, we slowly got up, grabbed our cups, and made our way somewhere else.

The city was both awake and sleeping. It was as if the people were zombies walking towards nowhere at all. Looking around me, I saw that no one was smiling. There was nothing to smile for. We were living in strange times. Cold times. Scary times.

Lies were being sold to the public. Dangerous lies. I wondered if we would ever be told the truth.

Like me, Sima also ignores most of what the mainstream media tell us. The media seems to have one agenda: the sale of fear. And a new form of racism seems to be slowly creeping in; an agenda against the straight white male, sponsored by the media and whoever owns it, but this is only an excuse to divide us. The billionaire villain(s) a.k.a. the Invisible Hand is turning us against each other, weakening us in the process, using its money to promote its agenda, using its money to make itself look like the hero/heroine of this story, but it's a lie. But the woke generation can't see past the lie. Instead they clap the villains. There are times when I feel as if we're living through the Last Days, slowly walking towards the End. And some of us are clapping. What the hell is happening to our world?

Sima agrees with me.

We find another place where we can sit down and resume our talk, just by the Herbert Gallery.

Young skaters are doing their thing (skating/tricks/falling over) not that far from where we are. Life goes on but for how long?

If people don't want your true love, don't try to force it on them. Instead, take a deep breath, smile (but keep the smile to yourself), walk away, remove yourself from those people's lives, and give it (your love) to someone who cares, who deserves it, and then, later, watch (not in surprise) as those who ignored you and laughed at you come running back to you, and when they do that and ask for your love back, just shrug your shoulders, give them a lame smile, and quietly say, "Sorry but I've moved on. I gave my love to someone who appreciates it."

If they aren't there for you on your bad times, why should you carry them through your good times?

It will come for you, to you; all that you asked for, all that you prayed for, the things you need, the dream you want to realise. A bit of hope (and faith) is needed, and a bit of patience, too. Just wait, a few months or so. You asked for it: He heard you, now wait, patiently, faithfully.

March 22nd. After a few hours" sleep, I shower, get changed, grab my long black coat, bought last year, another black coat for the collection, four of them, all bought on the sales, one of them actually cost me only five pounds, from a charity shop in Bath, and I also grab a small Bible, which I found somewhere ages ago, its spine damaged, and a notebook, and then I take the 6A bus to the city centre. I wanted to walk all the way there but I don't have much time left before I have to come home, grab my laptop and a few bits, and pick up Leaf from school. My life seems to be a constant race, destination nowhere or unknown, but I also have long periods of silence and stillness, so I can't really complain.

Inside the bus, I read Leviticus 25, a great chapter where the LORD tells us what to do, when, how, and why, but Mankind seems to be paying no attention to the Lord's word. It's no wonder the world is in such a mess.

There are four other people in the bus but I'm the only one who's reading. The other four are glued to their phones. This is a normal sight now; people constantly glued to their screens, especially in this New Age, the Age of Lockdowns and Social Distancing. Some people are forgetting what it means to be human but they don't seem to care. You'll be making your way down the street and you'll see someone walking on the opposite direction, and afterwards you or the other person will cross the road so that you won't have to walk past each other. The fear of humans is real. The fear has been forced upon us and it is now being disguised as the New Normal, labelled as the New Normal when there's nothing normal about it.

A billionaire software developer who, for some unknown reason, identifies himself as a doctor, scientist, and saviour of the human race, all rolled into one, is one of the sponsors of this New Normal, and he even wants us to eat synthetic meat and other crap, and the media, some scientists (how much money have they been given by this fake doctor?), and a lot of other people support this Machiavellian devious plan, but this is the opposite of what G-d want us to do. If it wasn't for the fact that I can make free calls on Signal and WhatsApp, I would have got rid of my smartphone ages ago and gotten myself a so-called dumb phone. Soon, I still might get one.

St. John 8:36

I got a chicken roll and a cup of coffee from the Baguette Bakery in Coventry Market. That's lunch out of the way. Both me and the bakery owner agree that we might have another lockdown on the way, maybe after summer. It never ends. Our so-called leaders work for someone else, for the real leaders, the profiteers of the New Normal. The media doesn't talk about these people; they're "invisible", and the reason why the media won't mention the "Invisible Hand" is because they're owned by them.

"…Ye shall seek me…"

Not so long ago, I wrote some sort of sci-fi novel where I mention the Invisible Hand, but not even I dare to say too much about them. After all, I don't want to be demonetized, erased, "killed". I too need to survive.

"…and shall not find me…"

Demon…etized; what a word. The first five letters of it tell you everything you need to know.

The Invisible Hand seems to worship Moloch above anything else, but I know better than that. Only a clean body can enter the Kingdom of God. Or should I say only a clean soul can enter the Kingdom of God?

I'm not perfect myself; I'll probably never reach perfection, but, like so many others, I know right from wrong; I know what I must do; I know what I should (and shouldn't) do, and I'm trying to live a clean life, a life close to perfection, perfection in the eyes of God and not in the eyes of Man.

Mankind seems to be rushing towards the end but why should I join the majority when they seem to be lost?

Scary times we're living in; I'm repeating myself but no one seems to be listening. The New Normal seems to be No Love, No Touching, Get Away From The Ones You Love, Don't Love, Keep Away, Keep Away, Keep Away; if you don't find this scary, I don't know what else to say.

I sit outside the market, on some steps that lead to closed shops. I eat, drink, watch, write. A lonely life but for now it is the life I must live. Later, who knows?

I read words that are centuries' old but these words never seem to age and they make more sense now than ever. I read because I'm searching for something; a way out, a way in, answers, salvation, redemption, but "time is running out" and I have to stop reading and head home, grab my bag, brush my teeth (again), and then get my daughter from school.

I put the Bible away, in one of my coat pockets; it's a small Bible so it fits there, and then I make my way to the bus stop. On the way there, I see a young Asian woman almost bump into a lamppost because she's glued to her iPhone and wasn't even looking where she was going. Some people are walking, eyes wide open, and they can't see. Scary, isn't it?

When I get home, the landlady is already up. She goes to bed late and gets up late. She's a quiet soul, scared of the New Normal. Needless to say, she hardly ever leaves the house and spends most of her time glued to a screen. The New Normal isn't normal at all. I wonder what Henry Miller or Tolstoy would make of the New Normal.

The New Normal is madness.

The New Normal is people barking at you when they disagree with you.

The New Normal is madness.

I grab my bag, leave the small Bible behind; I have another one in my bag, a bigger volume, and then I leave home. I decide to walk all the way to Earlsdon. A walk will do me good. Every day I try to go for a nice long walk. "They" want us to stay indoors at all times but the body needs fresh air, sunlight, life, Nature, and not to be glued to a screen at all times. The New Normal isn't normal at all.

Leaf tells me why she doesn't want to go to the house of Yu's friend on Sundays. Trish, Yu's friend, has two daughters, and whenever Leaf is alone with the other girls they bully her, make fun of her, and sometimes even kick her.

"Mama says they're my friends but kicking someone and bullying them is the opposite of friendship," Leaf says.

I nod.

In Yu's defence, if she knew this was happening she would go berserk. You can say whatever you want about her but she's a good mother.

"You no longer have to go there," I say to Leaf and hold her hand. "You can stay with me every Sunday or whenever your mother goes to her friend's house."

Leaf tells me not to tell a thing to her mother, and I nod, but later, when Yu is home, I take her aside and tell her everything. Yu doesn't know what to say. She's shocked, even hurt, but not surprised. She knows how cruel some kids can be, especially in their own environment, two against one.

"Trish did give me a funny look on Sunday when I turned up at her home alone. She asked about Leaf, but not about Matthew, and I told her Leaf wanted to spend time with her dad," Yu says.

We agree that from now on, whenever Yu goes to Trish's house, I'll stay at her place with the children.

A few minutes later, Yu is glued to her church's religious book, a book that was written by a serious polygamist. Like me, she's also looking for something, for faith, for a reason why, but maybe she's looking for it in the wrong place. Sadly, for such a religious person, Yu hardly ever touches the Bible.

We're one with G-D but some people get lost and forget that they're one with G-D. So what do they become?

An American friend of mine has told me that the real people running the United States is an unelected aristocracy (The Invisible Hand?) that believes the American people can't (and shouldn't) choose their own leaders and so it makes its own choice.

"This unelected elite who are calling the shots have now in power who they want; a real puppet who will obey every single order without complaining," he said.

I nodded, said nothing, letting, with that gesture of mine, my friend know that I agreed with what he was saying. I've written about this Invisible Hand before, but even though what I wrote about it was fiction, the Invisible Hand is real. It hides itself in the shadows, behind powerful agendas, it gives itself no name (but its agendas have various names), and it is very powerful.

"Some people wrongly believe that a revolution is the only way to bring the elite down but the elite controls the law, the media, the banks, hospitals, science, etc. How can a person even fight such a powerful enemy?" my friend Bernard said.

While he was telling me all that, I was thinking, "Here I am, still writing conspiracy tales."

But the conspiracy is real, at times unreal, and they call it conspiracy so that the majority of people get fooled and believe the LIE. We just have to look at monster Epstein and the people he dealt with, all powerful people; child abusers, blood drinkers, modern-day vampires, worshipers of Moloch, none of them, as of yet, punished by the law. How can they be punished (by the law) when they are the law?

Billionaire, self-proclaimed saviour of the world Will I-identify-as-a-scientist-and-doctor-though-I'm-neither Bates was friends with monster Epstein and now he's advising the entire world on how to fight this virus known as the Invisible Enemy but what credentials does he has as a doctor or scientist? None. Sometimes I wonder if Will is Moloch.

Seeing what's happening in the States frightens me a bit, and I must admit that the country is a mess, the wrongful agendas are being pushed forward, things like good morals and dignity seem to be almost extinct, and whoever is in control of the chaos (controlled chaos, created to fool you and control you) seems to want to extinct both G-D and religion. A New World is being created for us, for everyone, a New Age where love and good manners won't be allowed. Not even a hug or a smile will be allowed. Maybe Moloch is the one behind it all.

Moloch is mentioned in Leviticus 18:21 and again in Leviticus 20:2-4; something about giving or passing children to Moloch. It sounds like some sort of sacrifice of children, and, for years, I've heard rumours of such things still taking place in this modern age; sacrifice of children, and those rumours involve some powerful figures. Psalms 106:37-38 also mentions sons and daughters being sacrificed unto devils, innocent blood being shed, sacrificed unto the idols of Canaan.

Jeremiah 7:31 and Jeremiah 19:5 also mentions the sacrifice of children but Moloch isn't mentioned. But further ahead, in Jeremiah 32:35, Moloch is once more mentioned.

Many years ago, American radio show host Alex Jones (of Infowars) managed to infiltrate a restricted private area in California, which was being attended by important men. Images recorded by Alex and his cameraman Mike showed these important figures worshiping a statue that some people said was Moloch. Of course, most of the media didn't/doesn't bother to report this. It can't, can it? So they label it a conspiracy theory even though it is real, it happened, and you believe the LIE.

A strange world, spinning out of control, but the majority of people seem oblivious to it. Just the other day, on YouTube, I saw these soy boys, snowflake generation clapping and laughing in a disturbed manner while waiting for Dr Caucci to turn up for a Zoom meeting. It was so unreal, and so unmanly, like something out of a terrible comedy about to turn itself into a horror movie with a disturbing ending. Of course, the Fake News loves this and tries to make it more than what it actually is.

We live in a society where wrong is clapped and worshiped, and right is slowly being put aside or, worse, labelled wrong. This shows me that we live in a society heading towards the collapse. Oh yes, the collapse will happen. And afterwards we'll have to rebuild again. Nothing new there. My friend Saul agrees with me. He even said, "When the collapse happens, make sure you're not in the middle of it. Stay hidden, and later be one of those who rebuilds."

A frightening world, manipulated by evil minds.

The rock star is almost dead, the footballer plays for an empty stadium, the movie star is slowly turning into a small screen star. The true author is dead, or gone woke which is even worse than dying without a fight.

The world is slowly being turned into a virus that is covered by a long lie named face mask. I walk into a supermarket without wearing a face mask and everyone looks my way. I'm the new abnormal. As for everyone else, since they're wearing face masks (and obeying the LIE), they're the New Normal. Dr. Caucci is laughing alongside the soy flakes. Will Bates is sitting in his big ranch laughing his head off. Someone is playing a prank on us and you're clapping. The world is becoming a tragic comedy and only the chosen ones are allowed to laugh. A bored (and boring) author (I) boards a bus heading to the city centre. He's got no face mask on. Everyone's looking at him. Inside the bus, he sees a young man, probably a student, reading Chilean poet Nicanor Parra. The author quickly writes down the name of that poet. He's read him before, years ago, but he wants to remember the name and check him out again. It's such a cold day and he forgot his scarf at home. *Damn!*

April 2nd. The darkness (depression) sneaked in from behind me when I was at my lowest, recovering from more bad news; they never stop coming, the bad news that is; I pray and pray and pray, and pray a bit more, but everything I ask for seems to evade me and I only get what I don't want. I thought I was out of the darkness but am I still stuck in the Dark Night of the Soul? No, I don't think so.

I do feel as if I'm going through some transformation, leaving the old me behind and becoming someone else. I've mentioned this before, maybe in another book, maybe in my thoughts only, and I'll mention it here again; even my speech is slightly changing as I go through some sort of change. But who am I becoming? When will the transformation end?

I work with some strange people, almost heartless (people). Some of them have no dreams.

Some of them basically live for gossip and when someone else is down, they kind of feel happy. Strange people indeed.

There's this lad, whom I've worked with for close to 12 years, who loves nothing more than gossip and conflicts. Not once, during my separation, when I was at my lowest, and even now, did he asked me how I am, but if he happens to have a problem, no matter how small it is, he wants everyone to stop what they're doing and listen to him. Sad fella, but I've already written about him, in another book, so I won't mention him that much. Soon I need to move on, meet new faces, write something else.

Last Wednesday, Yu went on a date while I stayed at her place looking after our children. She told me that she was going out for a walk after work and I made nothing of it, but later, when I was in bed with my daughter Leaf, watching cartoons with her on her phone, something inside me told Yu was out on a date, and on the following morning I asked her if she'd been out on a date. I had fallen asleep before she arrived home, but even when I was sleeping that voice inside me told me more than once that Yu was on a date.

"Yes, I went out with someone, but it was a disaster and he didn't even wanted to go out with me," she said.

She also told me that her date was from a different religion, and I thought, "So, one of the reasons why you left me was because I'm from a different religion than yours, but you went out with someone that also belongs to a different religion. Hmm."

I came then to the conclusion that, when we met, I was never her first choice. I probably was her only choice.

I also realised that, unknowingly, she won't rest until she completely destroys her life and ends up completely alone. But she's no longer my concern. I don't hate her, but, as time goes by, I like her less and less.

For now, I carry my cross, a heavy cross, but it's getting lighter by the day, and one day (because karma is real and life isn't a beach) Yu will have to carry her own cross.

Yu told me she met him on a dating site and that she has already closed her account. I said nothing. There was nothing for me to say. When I thought about it, I was looking at a stranger, not at someone whom I once loved.

I lowered my cross and took a break. That voice inside me said, "One day, those who hurt you will be looking for you, looking for your forgiveness and your love, and they won't be able to find you. Only then will they realise the mistakes they have done. For now, carry your cross (better men have carried heavier crosses), but lower it, bit by bit; leave it behind, and wait. Better days will come. Just wait."

Maybe Father was right. Maybe I was too good for Yu. I gave her so much but she was never satisfied. Looking back now, at all those years I spent with her, I come to the conclusion that I probably should thank her for the divorce. She saved me from a nightmare; the nightmare that is her.

Yu went on another date, with some guy she met online. Two dates with the same guy. But even though she's going on dates, bit by bit her life is becoming a mess. She wants to quit her job and move somewhere else; another job that pays a lot less. And she even has to pay for car parking at this new place. Definitely a tragedy waiting to happen. But Yu never learns, and then she blames her mistakes on others.

The other day, when I was at her place looking after our children, she came home stressed from work. Minutes later, she said, "No one does a thing for me. It's like being married to you."

Another insult to add to the collection. I took it, swallowed my pride and anger ("And what the hell have you done for me, bitch? You bought a home behind my back and left me with nothing!" I felt like saying), and said nothing. For now, because of our children, I keep quiet, but one day I'll have my say. Actually, when that time comes, maybe I'll keep quiet. Too quiet. In fact, G-D willing, I might even "disappear". My entire self, body and soul, wants to leave Yu behind once and for all. One day, when our children are older, I don't want a thing to do with her.

Centuries ago, the greatest philosopher of all time, walked among us, taught us how to live a righteous life, showed us the Way, only to find Himself persecuted, trialled, tortured, and crucified. What chance do we have?

Actually, because of Him, our chances are quite good. And we must believe.

John 14:1

April 11th. Two days ago, again (LEAVE ME ALONE!!!), briefly, I was visited by the sadness, cried a bit, cried while going for a walk, cried because of the loneliness, cried because of the time that I spent away from my children, but I must be stronger, strong enough to start again. I have to let go of the things that are out of my control, let go of the past, and start again.

And I must stop crying.

My love is here, inside of me, ready to be given to those who deserve it, but, for now, I'm going to lock some of it away, keep it safe and not out there, in the open, and only give it when I see that that person deserves it.

April 15th. The year's still 2021.

Leaf's birthday. We play happy family and go to Solihull for the day. Yu drive us there, on the car that I bought with her, a car that is now hers. I'm a passenger. For now I'm a passenger. One day I'll be the one doing the driving but I won't have Yu sitting next to me. She doesn't know it yet but she's dead to me. For now, because of the children, I smile, only a bit.

For now, I endure, but one day...

She taught me how to hate. Maybe I should thank her for it.

Life goes on.

It does, doesn't it?

It must...

I must put away the sadness (and the hate) and move on.

Life is a show and the show must go on.

Create a house of prayer for yourself.

Create a house (of prayer) inside yourself.

Psalm 82:6

(Remember this)

24th April. I haven't written here in a long time. There isn't a lot to say, not much to write about.

I cried a bit.

Sometimes I still cry.

I cry because... because...

I cry because I miss my children.

I cry because I miss what I never had.

April 27th. I read somewhere online that the Dark Prince (Moloch) is already here. I must become like Shun Kaidou a.k.a. Jet-Black Wings and fight the enemy.

The Dark Prince's mission is the destruction of families, separate man from woman, turn us into something else. God created us male and female, but the Dark Prince wants to destroy God's creation. And the Dark Prince has a powerful tool to brainwash everyone; social media, the small screens that everyone uses.

It's a long battle and I have zero superpowers.

The family life needs to be saved but there's a powerful enemy that is trying to destroy it. Speak about it (and go against it) and you will be **demon**etized.

Thursday, 29th April. Life goes on, at a slow pace. Any slower than this and I'll turn into a turtle.

And while life goes on, at a slow pace, for me that is because others seem to be rushing nowhere, an on-going battle is being fought online, a battle between Right & Left, right and wrong, a battle of lies, fake news (and are both sides wrong?), racism, fear, and those who say they're right, they're actually wrong, so wrong, dead wrong, but they're sponsored by Powerful People (both sides?), sponsored by the Big Tech, sponsored by a Lie (and fear), sponsored by the Invisible Hand (all sides?), and even though some of them know that they're wrong, they don't care. Some of these people follow Moloch, not G-D.

And then there are others who don't even know that they're in a cult, following a lie, destroying the purity of the world.

This afternoon, before I went to get my daughter from school, I decided to get a couple of cupcakes from Greggs on Earlsdon Street, one cupcake for my daughter Leaf and another for her friend Kate, and after I paid for the cakes, I turned around and saw a man standing outside, face mask on, and when I stepped out of Greggs, the man shouted, "Shame on you for not wearing a mask!"

At first I didn't hear him properly, and so I followed him inside Greggs and asked, "Excuse me, but what did you say?"

He turned around (and I saw so much hate in his eyes, rage, a look that said he wanted to hurt someone, a look that said he wanted to fight, but maybe he was fighting the wrong enemy) and said/shouted, "Shame on you for not wearing a mask!"

I looked at that podgy, horrible, ugly face and decided not to let him upset me.

The man then leaned forward and saw that I was wearing a badge that said I was exempt from wearing a face mask and was quick to apologise, but the damage was already done and I saw him for what he clearly was; he was a fool, a fool with a loud mouth and a short temper.

After he apologised, I said, "Okay," and walked away.

In the past I would have lost my temper too, but I'm getting older, wiser, softer; calmer I should say, calmer because of G-D and Jesus and meditation and Kelly Howell's voice when I go to sleep.

I walked away (because what else could I do?), crossed the road, waited, and then crossed the road again, and sat outside Earlsdon Methodist Church for a few minutes where I read a few pages of Daniel Defoe's *A Journal of the Plague Year*. The man with the loud mouth didn't stay in my head for too long. I'm too old for those things, too old to let some idiot live in my head for too long. Bit by bit, since last year, I've been changing my way of thinking, but last week my mind started to leave even more stuff behind including friends who weren't really friends and events that no longer matter, and as my mind emptied itself of futile things, I saw that there was no point in getting mad about certain subjects or the actions of some people, and that's why when the man with the loud mouth was so aggressive towards me (and maybe he had his reasons to fear the Invisible Enemy; maybe he had lost someone to it, or maybe he was just scared; nothing wrong with that as we're all scared of something), my mind said, "Forget it." And that was it: "Forget it." Forget it and just walk away. The fool could fight itself and the world, but his fight wasn't my fight. The world is fighting itself and instead of bringing more hate to the table I'll try to bring some sort of peace.

Friday, 30th April. A bad day but I'm sort of okay now. What happened was, when I was at work, around 0:14AM, while I was doing a patrol, I felt sick, a bit dizzy, and so I returned to the security room where I sat down and thought, "If I just stay still, I might last until the end of my shift and then catch a cab home."

I sat down for a few hours, or maybe for less than two hours, but around 3AM I was dying to go to the bathroom and so I stood up and made my way out of the security room, but I'd only taken a few steps when I felt my body quit on me. Not only that but the whole room was spinning and I couldn't keep my eyes open. Seconds later, I was on the floor, eyes closed, the whole room spinning round. No matter how hard I tried, I couldn't keep my eyes open. Luckily there were other workers in the building so I called one; his name's Dave, told him I wasn't feeling well and that I needed help. He came downstairs to where I was, and after waiting a few minutes to see if I was going to recover, Dave decided to call for an ambulance. As for me, I could hardly move. I was dying for a pee but my body just wouldn't obey me and I had no strength left.

It didn't took long for the ambulance to arrive and before I knew it, I was on my way to the hospital where I was then put on a wheelchair, whisked around to a hospital room, and put on juice. My blood pressure was sky high and I still couldn't keep my eyes open.

I stayed at the hospital for hours. Later, Yu picked me up from the hospital. She told me that I could stay with her for a few days and that she'd spoken with my boss who told me to take 5 days off and then return to work. I didn't know what to say. Yu had managed to finish work early and now she was playing the role of the good ex-wife, but it wouldn't last. Anyway, I didn't have that much strength left, and I didn't really know what to say so I kept quiet. But even then, in the car, she was being bossy, at times, almost aggressive, but I couldn't be bothered to argue or fight.

Before I know it, I was at her place, and Matthew and Leaf were there too, and I thought, "I'm going to get to spend a few days with my children, play with them, laugh alongside them," but I forgot who I was dealing with. But everything that happened had to happen. I needed to say goodbye to Yu, again and again, for good, a long goodbye, see you later but only briefly, a goodbye that, unconsciously, I had been denying myself, not because I wanted to get back together with her but because I wanted to be near my children, but that goodbye had to happen so that I could start again.

At first, Yu played the part of the good ex-wife, the part of a caring person, but she's definitely going crazy and it wasn't long before she started to boss me around, saying that I wasn't that poorly even though I had spent hours in a hospital bed, and as I stood there listening to her as she shouted at me, I knew that I was wasting my time on her, with her, and so I grabbed my stuff and left her place. My boss called me when I was on the bus heading home, and I told him that I was fine and could go back to work on the following day. What happened was I had forgotten to take my medicine for quite a long time, for weeks I should say, but, hopefully, I wasn't going to make that same mistake. I said that to my boss but he told me to take the time off and rest.

When I got home, I sat in bed, looking at the ceiling, wondering when my life would actually change for the better. No matter what I did, no good changes seem to be coming my way. And I was getting so tired of everything. There were times when I felt as if I was dying, times when I felt like quitting. Meanwhile, while I was dying, Yu was probably in bed playing on her phone.

I closed my eyes and tried to go to my happy place, but where was that? The truth is I was lost, so lost, falling all the way down into the abyss, heading towards death.

I found myself crying.

I fell asleep while crying.

I cried even in my dreams.

I was tired.

I was tired of crying, tired from crying, tired of life.

When would things get better?

Tuesday, 18th May. What a few mad weeks I had, weeks where I thought about giving up, but give up what?

Everything…

But what do I have that I can actually give it up?

Dreams…

Faith…

Life…

Everything.

What happened was (I cried and I died, again and again, and I'm still dying, a slow death), what happened, was, what was, what… I fucking lost my mind! That's what happened.

After being five days at home, I returned to work. First night back at work, I caught a bad cold that would last for the five nights that I was on duty but I didn't miss a days' work. I couldn't because, for now, my job is all that I have and I just can't start missing shift after shift, so, sick or not, I went to work, stayed in the building on my own, moved my tired body up those long steps, wondering when life would improve, when would I get a break (and, in my head, I swore so much, night after night, I cursed), and on the fifth night, just as I was starting to feel a bit better, I eased down on my chair, closed my eyes for a few minutes, waited for the shift to come to an end, felt the sickness abandoning my body, felt better, a bit better, but then I went home, straight to bed, and I was only in bed for a few hours when I woke up, and my left eye was on fire, or it felt as if it was on fire, and I couldn't keep it open, and I thought, "No! Please, give me a break, Lord. I can't take this."

I got up, went downstairs, dragged my body down the stairs, downstairs, down, so down, and I washed my face, my eyes, but the itchiness, pain, darkness, depression, nothing would go away, nothing was helping, nothing, no help, no, no, no, no help at all, no one by my side, no one to call for help, and I went back to my room, up the stairs, poor body, keep on moving; if you stop you die, you're not allowed to rest, up, up, up, and then down, into the abyss, jump into the arms of the darkness, let depression take you away, no, no, no; I was going mad, yes, by then I was going mad, or maybe I have always been mad, a mad writer, a mad poet, the child of Baudelaire and Dostoevsky, or maybe the child of Sartre and de Beauvoir, the unknown child of Yukio Mishima, born in the West, born in London, born and abandoned, abandoned as a child, abandoned as an adult, abandoned and left to die, or reborn, reborn, be born again, my child, become a samurai (or am I going crazy?), become an author, find your happy place, find… I found my trainers, only one eye open, the left eye itching, burning, found my socks, found this and that (and I was so lost), went down the stairs, down, all the way down, kept on walking even though I was so tired, drained really, tired of everything, even life, especially life, life and love (or should I say life and lie because love is a lie, isn't it? haven't you read this book from the beginning? Didn't you read what I wrote?), and I took a bus to the city centre, a bus that would take me to Pool

Meadow Bus Station, and then I would make my way to the Walk-in Centre in Stoney Stanton Road, walk back and forth, don't rest, poor writer, don't rest and forget about love (because love is a lie), and when I got there I had to wait for a few hours, but that's okay because I don't need to rest, wait and wait, and then I was told I had an eye infection, nothing to worry about, some eye drops and I would be okay (but inside I was dying; is there a cure for that?), and so I bought the eye drops, made my way back to town, ate some shit somewhere, sat somewhere, alone, always alone, and then I went home, back to my bedroom where I sat alone, always alone, but I couldn't be at home. I needed to be out. I needed to die. I needed to breathe. I needed to live. I needed... Bloody hell, I'm so needy.

I went somewhere, sat on the grass, cried, prayed, went back home, cried, prayed with tears in my eyes, and then I took a break. How much can a person cry?

And because I was poorly for so many weeks, poorly and depressed, I didn't write a thing. For a while, I even thought about giving up my writing. And then do what?

Die...

Or start again.

Thursday, 20ᵗʰ May 202iiiiiiiiii. Life seems to have come to a stop. Again. I say again because this has happened before, but now, unlike yesterday (and by yesterday I mean in the past), I don't try to rush things or make sense of what's happening. Damn! Can anyone make sense of what's happening in the world right now?

Instead, I sit somewhere. And I might read or write. Or drink a cup of coffee and eat a sandwich. Then back to writing. Or reading.

This morning I came to Caffé Nero in the Lower Precinct, Coventry. I just wanted to get out of my bedroom and go out for a walk, sit somewhere, enjoy a cup of coffee, which I can do now because most shops are finally open, and write something. During lockdown, while I was going through my separation, everything was closed, and whenever

I was out, I couldn't sit at a café and write. The lockdown caught me at a terrible time, but life goes on.

Yesterday, I spent a few hours with my children at my ex-wife's place. At the moment, because of my conditions (HELP ME, LORD!!!!!!!!!!!!), I'm a part-time father, meaning I only have my children for a few hours every once in a while and not as much as I would like. Every minute spent with them feels like gold; so precious, but I don't like to go to their mother's home. Her home reminds me of a house I left behind in the town of Portimão, a house of nightmares, a house that gave me nightmares, a house that, finally, is starting to become a distant memory. But if I want to see my children, I have to go to Yu's place, and sometimes I have to grit my teeth when she says something stupid, something aimed at me, which she does quite often, or orders me around, which she tries to do quite often.

Yesterday I've noticed that Yu's becoming quite ugly. Maybe the ugliness comes from inside, from within, and it's starting to spread on the outside. I've realised too late that she's a selfish person; she takes and takes, from everyone, and when that person has nothing else to give her, she cuts ties with them. She likes to arrive home and have everyone running after her or doing things for her while she sits her fat arse on the sofa. She's a vampire and I believe that she doesn't even know it.

Two days ago, she came home after work, told me she was going out again to get some shoes for our daughter and a takeaway for all of us, including me, and then she went out again, with our daughter, while I stayed at her place with our son, and she returned a while later, with no food, no food for any of us, and before I could say something she told me she had an online meeting and that she was busy and that I could go out and get some food for myself and the kids, but nothing for her because she already had some dinner ready for her in the fridge; only for her but not for the children, and then she sat her fat arse on the sofa, smartphone in front of her ugly face, and that was it. No one was allowed to ask her any questions or interrupt her. The Snake, I mean Queen, actually, I mean Snake, the Snake wanted silence and that was it.

I swallowed my pride and went out, walked past her car, which used to be our car, bought some food for me and the kids, and while I was waiting for the food it started to pour down, and then I made my way back to Yu's place.

My trousers were wet, my trainers were wet, my socks were wet, and as I was making my way back to Yu's place, I had some sort of Revelation. A voice inside me said, "What are you doing? Why do you keep chasing people that don't deserve your time, never mind your love?"

And then I started to relive the past, and I saw Yu screaming at me, always putting me down, bossing me around, giving the cold shoulder, and when I arrived at her place, completely wet, I dropped the food on the table, said, "Here's your dinner, children," and then I left.

I was tired, hurt, wet, my chest was hurting, and I just wanted to sit down, eat something in peace, and then go to sleep.

I waited close to one hour in the rain for the next bus to arrive, and when I finally got home, I got changed, ate something, washed my face, brushed my teeth, said my prayers, and then went to bed. I love my children but I also need to love myself and take care of my body and my mental health.

Yu texted me shortly afterwards on Telegram. She wanted to know why I left so suddenly, and then she said that the four of us should go out next week for dinner, pay halves, etc., but what she doesn't know is that I don't want to spend another minute with her. For now, as I've mentioned before, because of our children, I have to see Yu, but one day, the moment I get the chance, I will cut her out of my life, completely.

Yesterday I met Cassio in town, outside the Holy Trinity Church, but only briefly. He returned me £20 that I had lent him and he still owes me £20. And afterwards, instead of going home and save some money, he went to Coral to gamble. No wonder he's always broke.

Cassio tires me out as he's constantly gambling, losing, and then he calls me to ask me for money. Last week he called me to borrow twenty pounds for tobacco. And the week before he called to borrow the same amount. And afterwards he spends the little he has gambling. Or he buys junk from charity shops. But he forgets that other people also need money and that we also have our own expenses and, in my case, other mouths to feed. He's my friend, and he doesn't have a lot of people left that can help him, but I wish he could save a bit more. What will he do one day when people like me move away? Who will he borrow money from?

A day of nothingness. Maybe a life of nothingness.

Once I leave Caffé Nero I go to H&M where I buy nothing, and from there I head to the Coventry Cathedral. After the end of my marriage, Christ became some sort of refuge for me. During that time, while I was going through my separation, the lockdown, divorce, pain, etc., I read and reread the New Testament a few times. And the Old Testament, too. I was looking for some sort of answers in the Word of G-d, looking for a reason why. I found something but I don't know what.

Something (someone?) inside of me, or around me, told me to keep on living, write, and forget the past. And repent.

Love passes you by and you wonder when you will love again/if you will love again. Or is Love a Lie, a Trap, Lust?

The writer is dead. Or slowly dying.

I don't know what to do with my life.

I'm sick of waiting for better changes to come my way, changes that seem to take forever.

I need it now, today, right now; a miracle, something from the gods, something that will allow me to live a better life, have my children with me, something…

Love?

Love is a lie.

I was lied to.

Love is a lie.

Don't you believe me?

You better believe it.

You better believe me.

Then again…

The phone hardly ever rings, which, in a way, is good because when people call me they only want to brag about their lives, what wonderful lives (and wives) they have, but all I hear are lies. Everyone is lying, mostly to themselves, not to me. And why are they telling me about their wonderful lives, their wonderful wives, their wonderful lies? Pathetic. Everyone is trying to compete with stupidity. Like I've said, pathetic.

I wait for some positive news to come my way; an email, a call, a text message; I need something, someone (love?), but nothing is coming my way.

I pray, to the skies, (to whom?), I pray and I ask (and I get down on my knees and beg) (and I think I might be going mad), but nothing, nothing, nothing.

I sit on cold steps, dirty steps, alone, away from the rain, from the world, from love (and where is love?) (where is the love?) (who killed love?) (Yu?) (Yu killed love), away from a lot of stuff but not from the cold, and I write and I cry and I wait, and nothing.

Oh Lord, hear my prayers.

Help me.

Please.

I create my own prayers.

I speak to an Invisible Being.

And then I wait…

For what?

Please, help me.

I need a home, my own place, a place where my children can come and stay with me, a place of my own, a place where I can pray, repeat, repent, a place where I can write my dreams, forget my nightmares, a place where I can have my desk, where I can read Stepanova, Bolaño, Sontag, Baudelaire, Ōe, Murakami, and where I can create a new life, forge a new path.

I need, Lord.
Please help me.
I need the Lord.
Help me, please.

The cold wind blows against my bare neck. I left my scarf at home.
I sit near Coventry Market, on some dirty steps, away from the rain.
I left my umbrella at home.
What's wrong with me?

21st May

The fear…
The fear of not knowing if I will ever love again.
The fear of not knowing if I will ever have my home, of not knowing if my children will ever live with me again.
The fear…
Change your thoughts and the fear will go away.

I come to the city centre, to Ed's Café at the Coventry Market, for a cup of coffee. As of yet I can't stay too long in that room that I'm renting. I feel trapped there, as if I can't breathe. The other two people living in the house are okay but I need to be alone. And I need someone.

Love dies; it gets killed by one of the partners, sometimes by both partners, and then you find yourself living with loneliness.

I slept for less than four hours.

I fell asleep while listening to Kelly Howell on my phone. For the last year I've been falling asleep while listening to her.

Love dies and afterwards I listen to Kelly Howell in my sleep.

Kelly has a good voice. I need a woman with a voice like hers, a Zen woman, a companion.

Love died but my heart is still beating, still searching for it, for love, not pain, no more (pain), please, still searching for that lie or for that feeling called love.

Yu doesn't know what love is.

To her love is gimme, gimme, gimme, but she's got it all wrong. Love should be, "Come closer, wrap your body around mine, put your arms around me, let me hear your heart beat."

Yu might never know that feeling. That is so sad.

Love is a feeling. And a lie.

Some people choose to feel.

Some people choose to lie.

I saw my daughter for twenty minutes today. Better than nothing, I guess. Better...

I didn't see my son, but I saw Yu the Snake.

I picked up my daughter from school, then waited outside, by the bus stop, for Yu to arrive from work. She finishes early on Fridays.

A cold day, raining most of the time.

A cold city, devoid of love.

I watched Yu arrive, a cold woman, devoid of love, park her car on the other side of the road, and then Leaf and I crossed the road. I helped my daughter get in the car. Her mother said something but I couldn't hear her. The truth is I can barely look at her. She makes me sick. Her face makes me sick.

Love dies and turns into sickness.

For now I must wait.

I'm waiting on news of an apartment, something affordable, waiting for my stories to be accepted (and published) by someone, waiting on better days, but nothing seems to be coming my way.

For now I must wait, and while I'm waiting, some people are laughing at my misery, making fun of me behind my back, laughing but why? What sad lives these people must live. What cruel hearts they must have.

I wait but I'm getting tired. And depressed. But I must wait. And while I'm waiting I must change my thoughts.

Yu is dead.

She's alive but she's dead.

In my heart she's dead.

Christ forgives.

I forget.

But I too must forgive.

Love dies but life goes on. People still write books. And love poems. And love songs. But the world is changing. The hate is growing. Most of the people wear masks, invisible masks, face masks, horrible masks, and if you're not wearing one, they give you the evil eye.

I wear no mask.

Love dies but the poet still feels compelled to write about it. Dan Brown is smart. He never writes about love. Not me. I feel compelled to tell you that love is a lie. What is wrong with me? Why can't I write a thriller like Dan Brown?

Love dies and I waste ink and time just to tell you that love is a lie.

I waste three hours in town, sitting on some footsteps that lead into a building, next to Bean & Leaf Café. The rain never stops falling.

Five women walk past me, smoking, talking, all dressed up, ready for a night out. I'm not a night person. Even though I work nights, I'm more of a morning person. If I could I would work on the day and then spend my nights at home. With love. Yes, that would be wonderful (but lately wonderful has been absent from my life); to work days and then spend the evenings at home, with love.

A man approaches me while I'm sitting down, asks me for some change, and I tell him I've got none. Seconds later, a woman approaches me, asks me for some change, and I tell her I've got none. Later, I see them together, hiding from the rain, smoking crap.

Psalms 6

The other day I saw a mother crying inside McDonald's. Little tears, little sobs. She had no wedding ring. Love dies and the ring gets sold. The child said something to his mum. I got closer to them because I wanted to hear what was being said. I heard the mother say, "You'll see your father in a couple of weeks."

I saw her wiping the tears of her eyes, her long thin fingers drumming on the table. Her coffee was getting cold. It looked untouched.

Love dies and you lose your appetite. It is as if love, or the loss of it, takes something from inside of you, a little box where you can store food, and once you lose love the thought of eating almost makes you want to puke.

Later on that same day, I saw a couple arguing outside Lidl. The woman was shouting, saying she had enough, while the man held on to the trolley. She got in the car and slammed the door behind her. The man sighed and put the empty trolley away. Then he quietly got in the car and slowly shut the door behind him. I watched them as they drove past me. The woman's face was pure rage while the poor man looked resigned to his faith.

Love dies and we go to war. Or one of us decides to become a monk. Om...

Saturday, 22nd May

This morning I only got a few hours' sleep. The story of my life for the last few years. And Yu wanders why I'm tired. And talking about that snake; I saw her this morning (and she saw me too). I was making my way to the bus stop when she drove past me in what used to be out car. She waved at me, as if nothing had ever happened, and I lazily waved my hand in the air before turning my back on her. And then I kept on walking, towards Earlsdon, instead of waiting for the next bus.

I went to Cassio's home for lunch. Every once in a while he invites me over to his place and if I can, I pay him a visit. Cassio's happy to see me. I sit on the sofa while he finishes cooking lunch. The news is on. Now that the Invisible Enemy is becoming old news the media is turning its attention to the eco-agenda. Once more fear will be sold to the world, and the majority of people will fall for the lies of the media. The world is damaged, because of greed, because of the power that a few people have. "Dirty" billionaire Will Bates was one of the faces behind Project Fear but now that he's going through a divorce (and a lot of people want to know why he was such good friends with dead monster Jeff; maybe Will is a monster too) Will has gone really quiet. For some reason (profit?), Will loves to sell fear, to use his billions to sell fear and to present himself as some sort of saviour, but I never liked him and always saw something underneath that nice guy image. What about those in the media who took his money and helped him to sell fear? They too are guilty.

After lunch, me and Cassio take the 21 bus back to the city centre. Cassio says he wants to go for a walk but the moment we're in town he heads straight to Paddy Power to gamble. He still owes me 20 pounds and he also owes 10 pounds at the Portuguese minimarket, and in a few weeks' time he has to go to Manchester to renew his Portuguese ID, but instead of saving money for the trip and pay back what he owes me, he heads to the machines and I watch him lose 10 pounds. And just when I thought things couldn't get worse, I watch him insert a 20 pound note in the machine.

I say, "No! Cassio, don't do that!"

But it's too late.

In the end he does gets his money back but I'm sure that later, maybe even today, he'll go back to the machines. And while I'm there waiting for him I realise that I need new friends. I need to hang out with other people and leave people like Cassio behind. He's not a bad person but he's a loser and it's only a matter of days before he calls me to ask for more money. But this time I will have to say no.

Isaiah 41:10

The world never stops.

G-d never stops.

We don't see Him (at work) but He's there, working.

Writer Elaine Kingett is looking for love. She's 71 but still looks good.

Love, true love that is, is ageless. And priceless.

I wonder how old Megan is now. And is she still alive?

(Megan was an old lover of mine, a former lover, decades older than me.)

Sunday, 23ʳᵈ May

I'm back at St. John the Baptist church. I came here yesterday just for a quick prayer but it has been a while since I came to mass. I think for now, unless something changes, I'll stick to this church. Yesterday afternoon, after Cassio and I went our separate ways; he went home or maybe he went back to Coral to gamble while I stayed at Caffé Nero for a bit longer, I came to the conclusion that I need new friends, that I need to meet new people, a certain type of people, so that I can start a new life. Now it's up to me to choose what kind of people I want to hang out with and what kind of life I want to live. And even though Cassio is a good friend, he's not the sort of person that I want to hang out with all the time. He's got no plans, no ambition, no desire to improve his life, not even a tiny bit. Of course I won't abandon my friend, but I also need to be a bit more selfish and think of me.

I'm getting rid of some of my notes and even some of my notebooks. I've got so many of them (notes and notebooks), written throughout the decades, written in Portuguese and English, but mostly in English. I take a couple of old notebooks to work, and some notes in loose sheets of paper, so that I can copy what I want to keep and afterwards I shred it all. Some secrets will remain untold, unwritten.

London 1999. The last year. Soon I'll be heading back to Portugal. I have some unfinished business there, some old faces to see, something waiting for me, maybe nothing. Another lost year, probably.

I'm at a café somewhere in Clapham Junction with Achy and a couple of her friends. Her friends talk too fast and they're so loud. Achy can tell that I hate being here. She rests her right hand on m left knee and gives it a slow squeeze. It's her way of telling me to be patient. And because I know that later we will have sex I wait. I wait for sex, not for love.

Sunday, 25th March 2021. I can't believe what I'm reading. I didn't even know I'd written this. I waited for sex, not for love. That's where I went wrong for so long; I waited on the wrong thing. But later I met Yu and gave her my love. She took everything and left me with nothing. Oh well, live and learn.

I go back to my old notes

London 1999. One of Achy friends, Milagros, seems to have it in for me. First, when I try to join the conversation, she tells me that my

Spanish isn't that good, and later she sighs when I say I still haven't read Borges. Yes, she really seems to have it in for me. But when I pay close attention to what she's saying, I realise that she complains a lot about other people; she's a moaner, not an achiever, and she blames her faults and problems on others. Listening to her talking really tires me out. I excuse myself and head outside for a cigarette. My ears need a break from all the moaning. Eugenia, another friend of Achy, is smoking at the table while her boyfriend Scott looks like he's about to fall asleep. (As I type down these notes of the past, I wonder what happened to all these people, where are they now, what are they doing?)

The moment I'm standing outside, breathing in the pollution, I feel like heading somewhere else, maybe Chinatown, for something to eat, but I wait on Achy. I wait for her lustful body. On the other side of the road a man is preaching about G-d and salvation but no one is really listening to him. No one listens until it's too late. I finish smoking but then I remain outside, writing notes in one of my notebooks. And while I'm writing I feel an urge to go somewhere else, a quiet place, and start working on a novel whose subject will be life, but, as of yet, I seem to lack the discipline to become an author. And so I wait, on Achy, on discipline, on dreams, on life, on love, on… on and on…

Coventry, 2021. This afternoon I bumped into a woman I've seen before. Every few Sundays I help out at a food bank, giving food and clothes to the homeless, and that's how I met this woman whose name I still don't know. She came over to where I was and we started talking, just me and her, a few metres away from everyone. It was close to 2PM and the area was already packed with people who were waiting to be fed. She didn't stay for too long. She'd just finished work, or was on a break, or whatever; I forgot. A pretty blonde, blue-eyed, yellow teeth; she's a heavy smoker; the short time she was with me she smoked two cigarettes. She stood really close to me, our bodies almost touching, her blue eyes never leaving my brown eyes. Like me, she refuses to have a vaccine against the bullshit, I mean, against the Invisible Enemy. I already like her. She told me she's a Guardian; basically she lives in a house, almost rent free, and looks after it. I could tell she's a bit of a wild spirit, maybe too wild for me, but the few times I met her we always enjoyed a good talk. Later at night, when I was already at work,

I found myself thinking about her, wondering how she is as a lover, and is she the kind of woman who would stay faithful to one man? Not that I fancied her; I don't; it's just the way my mind works.

The phone rings. A quick call from my brother Carlos. He does this quite often; gives me a call and puts the phone down, then waits for me to call back. Later, another missed call. This time is Cassio. A few minutes go by, another missed call. Cassio again. Later at night, another quick call, two rings, before the phone goes quiet. Carlos this time.

My friend Cassio and my brother Carlos think I'm either rich or earn loads, especially my brother Carlos because he's always giving me quick rings before putting the phone down, and if I call him back, month after month, he repeats himself, a bit like me when I write. He will say something like, "Me and my wife are both working. We earn good, we have a good life," or, "My wife has a new car," or, "We've been married for 25 years and…" and some other crap. At times I think that my brother is either stupid or involved in some sort of competition with me. He knows I'm going through a difficult time, with my divorce and everything, but he's always bragging about his life, every single time, or most of the time, especially now that I'm going through a depressive period of my life, and, whenever I call him or whenever he calls me, there are times when I feel as if he sort of envies me, which makes no sense because I have nothing. And more than once, after I had spoken to him, I got either bad news or something bad happened to me. Nowadays, whenever I get a missed call from him, I hardly ever call back, and if he calls me I don't always answer the phone. He wants to know everything so that afterwards he can go on a gossip rampage but I've learned my lesson and so now I either ignore the missed calls or tell him as little as possible. But, to be honest, there isn't a lot to say. Instead I will leave a few notes behind for some people to read (and decipher). Or I'll write a bad novel with the notes that I have.

Tuesday, 25ᵗʰ May. My son Matthew is feeling a bit poorly, so, after the end of my shift, I went home, got changed, bought some food from Sainsbury's in Canley, and then took the 6A bus to Yu's place. She's at work while Leaf's at school. I spent the whole morning with my son, slept for a couple of hours on Leaf's bed, got up, washed my face, took a bus back to town, picked up Leaf from school, back to Yu's place, played with Leaf and Matthew, cooked dinner for them, played a bit longer with Leaf, and when Yu got home, a few minutes past 8PM (was she on a date? Who cares? I don't...), I kissed my children goodbye, made my way to the bus stop, saw that the next bus would only be there at 9PM, so I went to a takeaway shop, bought a lamb kebab and a can of Dr Pepper, and then ate the food and drank my drink while waiting for the bus to arrive. When I got home, after brushing my teeth and washing my face, I sat on a chair reading *The Life of Saint Teresa of Ávila by Herself*. And while I was reading, I missed having someone by my side, a woman whom I could talk to, a friend, someone, but, for now, as love slowly resurrects, I must wait.

26th May. I just read about Annabelle Astley on the Mirror. Annabelle has Mayer-Rokitansky-Küster-Hauser syndrome, a congenital condition that includes having a shortened vagina, no cervix and no uterus, which means she will never be able to carry her own children or even have a period. Anyway, not so long ago she was brave enough to have an intimate relationship with a man, only for the idiotic fool to betray her and tell everyone in her university accommodation about her condition. What a loser. Why would you do something like that to another person, especially a young lady whom you just slept with? I'm glad to read that she dumped him on the spot. She deserves someone better. She deserves love. But isn't love dead?

This morning I sinned against G-d. I used my body for pleasure, for dirtiness, and I watched dirty images, the likes I promised never to watch again. I broke my promise, the promise I'd made to G-d. Once more I hope He forgives me and that He gives me another chance. In my defence (but how can I even defend myself?), I was lonely, the flesh got weak, followed my thoughts, and then my corrupted mind led me towards the Sin. Nevertheless, no matter how I put it, that is no excuse for what I have done. I should know better and I should do better and I will do better. And until then I won't ask a thing of G-d, or so I say but I bet it won't be long before I ask this and that.

After the sin was done I felt so ashamed. I know a lot of people who would say, "Don't worry about it. What you did is a natural thing," but I know better than that, and because I know better I should do better.

I took a shower, a long shower; the first attempt to cleanse the dirt out of my body and out of my soul. But the soul needs more than that, a lot more, so, afterwards, I said prayer after prayer. I will clean the body. And the soul.

I will.

I must.

Oh Lord, forgive me.

I am weak.

Forgive me, Lord, for my weakness.

For the past few months I've been reading a lot of books written by saints of the past and watching documentaries about monks and Tibetan Buddhists. My mind longs for something else; a change, a peacefulness that first must come from within. At the same time I want a woman with whom I can have long nights of passion. And I can have both; the long nights of passion and the peacefulness within. I've had them both before, when I was a young man, but only briefly, and, at that time, I didn't even know what I was looking for. And now, that I'm a lot older, I must put on my trekking boots and resume my search.

Help me, Lord, to get where I want.

Guide me so I won't get lost.

This world is nothing, only a passage to the next world, a path to Hell or Heaven, an entrance to the darkness or peaceful light, nothing at all, but right now the world is in turmoil, and the people are fighting against one another, being led to the slaughter by an Invisible Hand, and the Word of God is slowly being forgotten, even erased from some online sites. Scary times ahead, and this is only the beginning. I may not be the cleanest of persons, and I'm certainly no angel, but even if I die (and go to Hell) I will still keep the Word of God with me.

I can only write a bit of what I want to write. If I were to write everything that I want to write I would be persecuted, hunted like a dangerous criminal even though I haven't done anything wrong. But these are strange times we're living in; a time when wrong is right, when black is white, when a man of morals isn't allowed to say much. A Dark Force has taken over most ways of communication and the majority of people are being brainwashed by what they see, read, and listen. Only certain people become rich and famous but that fame and richness comes with a heavy price. Twerk, get naked, sell your soul, and you will become rich and famous. Good thing I don't want to be famous although I wouldn't say no to a few more bucks in my bank account. But there's only so much I would do for money. And a person shouldn't disrespect G-d, no matter how much money we're offered. But this Dark Force that is now in control of (mostly) everything has no mercy and it wants to corrupt the minds of everyone. I see people of all races, different faiths, damaging their bodies, destroying G-d's creation, and being applauded for it. There are many people who repent, and then, thanks to the Lord, and thanks to a New Found Faith in Christ, return to the people they used to be (and become Children of God Again), but you hardly ever hear about these people, the reason being the fact that this Dark Force controls most of what you see, read, and listen to, and if you want to know the Truth, and become a Child of God Again, you must leave a lot of things behind, even some friends and family members, and seek the Word of God. Travel alone, if you must, but, with G-d, you're never alone.

The Devil is real, but so is G-d. Now it's up to you to choose who you want to follow.

Yesterday, while lost in my thoughts, I imagined parts of Hell as a dark corridor where a person is forever lost in darkness. Wherever you look you see nothing but darkness.

This morning I got lost in sin but I regret it straight away and prayed for forgiveness. A few minutes before 12PM, I went to St. John the Baptist Church to say the Holy Rosary. If I'm strong enough, faith will save me.

There were only six of us at church. From there I went to Marks & Spencer where I bought the cheapest sandwich I could find and a smoothie. This is my life now, a life where sometimes I feel as if I'm chasing nothing (or too much of everything) (or something that will always slip through my fingers), but deep inside I feel as if things are changing for the better. But whatever good things come my way I'm going to keep quiet about it.

For the last few months I've been living a quiet life, a life of secrecy, a life of doing and not telling a soul about it, and this is the way I see myself living my life from now onwards. There's so much jealousy and envy around me, especially from those who supposedly love me, and if in the past I used to share my happiness with others, now I shut myself, like a clam.

I'm trying to get my own place, my own apartment, either that or a studio, through the council, and I have someone helping me, but I haven't told anyone about it. And I'm still writing loads but, apart from a few books, most of what I will write will be published under different names. I want privacy, a quiet life, not fame and the jealousy of others pursuing me.

I want a life of going to church, see a few friends, some family members, grow my own vegetables, travel a bit, read loads, and, most of all, spend a lot of time with my children. I don't even want for Yu to know a lot about my life. The only way to achieve that is probably by not sharing too much with my children either because then they might tell her about my life. She made her own bed, and pushed me out of it, so now I must find a better bed to sleep on. And a better woman to share my life with. Everything will come to me in due time. Or so I hope. If I doesn't, it doesn't…

I just have to be patient, a bit more patient, and trust the Lord. Unlike others He has never let me down.

Let's face it; no one is immune to setbacks. What happened happened (and now, looking back, I see that it happened for the best), and now I must focus on the present and make plans for the future. Redirect the mind, change my thoughts. And I'm already doing that (although there are days when I still feel a bit down, a bit depressed, just a bit sad, ready to quit) but I make sure to keep some of my plans secret. Hardly a soul needs to know what I'm doing with my life. People want to know just for the sake of knowing, and a lot of them hope to see you fail or they get jealous when you succeed. Their lives are so petty and empty that they envy those who go out in search of their dreams. Ignore the jealous ones; put them aside for good if you have to, banish them from your life, and believe in yourself. The secret is to look on the positive side of things and to forget the negative side. Right now I miss my children so badly, so bad that I cry, but I still see them quite often, four to five times a week, sometimes less than that, a lot less. I wish I could see them all the time but that's not possible, but I also can't be constantly thinking about them or feeling sad about the fact that they're not living with me. My time with them will come one day, maybe soon, pretty soon. And pretty soon, because of karma, faith, nature, a Higher Being, whatever, whomever, Life (and the World) will reach the end of a cycle and a new Cycle will begin. And I will jump on board and smile at Life because Life will be smiling at me.

I can't really complain about my life. In this strangest of times I'm still working; I kept on working throughout the lockdown, and I'm living a quiet life, a life spent at work, home, in coffee houses or in parks where I sit down to read and write. There are a few things missing in my life but I'm working on them, working for them, and the only person who can stop me is me alone.

Everything starts in the mind, with a thought.

There's light at the end of the tunnel. Visualise what you want, open your eyes and your mind. Yes, open your mind. Everything starts in the mind, with a thought.

May, 26th

Mother called me yesterday. Day by day she's gathering her strength back. Last year she had a battle with cancer, a battle that put her on a wheelchair, but bit by bit she's getting her strength back. And she's already walking, going places, but slowly. We spoke about life, breakups, divorces, distance, love, a love that never dies no matter the distance, Yu, snakes and poison, Carlos, greed and envy (see where I'm going?), and she told me that even though she loves Carlos, like me she also finds it had to have a proper conversation with him. I told her he had given me a few missed calls throughout the week but I no longer bother to call him back like I used to do. She too, bit by bit, is keeping low contact with him. Whenever we call him, or whenever he calls us, Carlos speaks a lot but says little that is worth listening. He repeats himself, talks about subjects that we care little for, gossips a lot about so-and-so but he forgets that both Mother and I don't even know who so-and-so is or we no longer know them that well. I've already talked about this subject, repeatedly, and here I am, repeating myself, just like my brother Carlos does. But I love my brother. Of course, I love him.

Mother would like for me to move to Spain one day, and I wouldn't mind moving there too, get myself a small house with a bit of land, and maybe even have my children and one of my brothers living with me, but if I stay in England, and get my own place here, that's fine too. I like it here. I like this country. I was born here and wouldn't mind dying here. Not now but much later.

A few weeks ago, when Mother told Carlos that she would like for me to move to Spain one day, Carlos phoned Father straight away and said, "M÷ is moving to Spain!"

And a few days later Father called me to ask if that was true. The problem with Carlos is that he hears something (but doesn't really "hears it") and then twists it around. And he can't know a thing.

I told Father that I wasn't moving to Spain, not yet, but no one knows what the future has in store for us. Later, I told Mother not to tell too much about our lives to Carlos.

I love my brother but he can't know much about my life. And since this is a time for new beginnings maybe I need to cut off my brother from life, not completely but only a bit.

Yesterday, while I was at Yu's place with our children, waiting for her to arrive home from work (but she'd gone somewhere else after work and it was already getting late), I felt a bit dizzy, almost to the point of passing out. I hadn't eaten much all day and, because of it, my body was suffering. When Yu finally got home she was upset because I hadn't done dinner for the children, but I was at her place, and last time I had cooked something for her and the children in her kitchen she got upset. I can never win with her. (But I can. I can win. I can win by ignoring her, by putting her aside.)

"I was waiting for you. I thought you were coming home straight after work," I said.

"I told Matthew I was going somewhere for a walk. Didn't he tell you?" she said.

"No," I said.

Her face was fuming. What the hell was her problem anyway? She'd probably been out on a date, another failed date to the collection, and she was taking out her anger on me. I was too tired to fight, sick of arguing with her, so I said nothing.

She dropped me at McDonald's. I got a meal for me and the children. Afterwards she dropped me at the bus stop close to the house where I live. And that was it.

And that's enough.

Yu no longer cares about me (or about anyone else but herself) but that's fine.

In the past I used to complain about her coldness so now why should I want to be with her? I need love, not coldness.

I was so hungry that I sat by the bus stop and ate my meal.

I was so hungry that my hands were shaking, but after some fries and a Big Mac down my throat, I felt a lot better. Then I washed it all down with some Coke.

When I got home I went straight to bed.

I woke up around 5AM, had some breakfast, but instead of staying up and rush around doing nothing, I went straight to bed. No more running after people. I need to look after number one. I need to look after myself.

In a way I'm in debt to poisonous Yu. She set me free. Now I need to "rewire my brain", be more positive about life and dreams, and just go for it.

It's never too late to change your brain. Or your life. Even success can be achieved later in life. People like Henry Miller, Morgan Freeman, and so many others are proof of that. The problem is, instead of changing (and really going for it), many of us spend our lives thinking about the past and failure. Forget the past and yesterday. Move on. Change your thoughts and the rest will follow.

I have lunch at a café inside Pool Meadow Bus Station. One of those old cafeterias that are becoming a rarity. In the past I didn't frequent this type of place, now I avoid the so-called Big Chains and I rather go to a family cafeteria. I order fish, chips, peas, salad and a bottle of water, pay for it at the counter, and then I sit to read and write. An older man is discussing Manchester United's loss to Villarreal last night with a young man. An old lady, maybe in her seventies, is drinking tea and doing the crossroads. I open Machiavelli's *The Prince*, read a few pages, and afterwards I write a few notes in my journal. A young man, foreigner, steps out of the kitchen and walks past me a couple of times. He's looking at the books that I have on the table. They are *Rewire Your Brain* by Shauna Shapiro, *The Prince* by Machiavelli, *The Lamplighters* by Emma Stonex, and *The Life of Saint Teresa of Ávila by Herself*. Ten minutes later, the same young man brings me my food. He says hello and smiles. I thank him and he says, "Enjoy your meal."

I eat the chips first, not bothering to use a fork, and while I eat I read.

A young woman walks past the café and smiles at me when our eyes meet. I smile back. Then back to reading.

After a while I put the book away and concentrate on my meal, but while I'm eating I'm also thinking, planning, designing a New Life for Myself. The Change(s) start Inside. For It to Happen the Brain must need a floor plan, a Design, a Plant for the Building. I have a spark of the Creator inside of me. That spark is all I need for a New Beginning, a New Life. I see it in the Mind; it's out there, just waiting for me. It wants me too. It longs for me like a starved lover.

I dreamt I was a father again. Married again, to a Jewish woman with short hair, a father to her child. I've seen this woman before, in another dream. Is she real? Is she out there, looking for me? And if she is (looking for me) am I ready to marry again?

Love again?

Trust again?

Become a father again?

Again...

...and again...

We sat in the back of her car smoking Marlboros because Marlboros was what she smoked while I smoked red Ducados but I'd run out of cigarettes so she gave me one of hers. A dark night. Cold but not that cold. A starry night. A night where I felt as if we were the only two people left in the world.

We were in the woods, close to the beach, naked, inside her car, naked and stoned, inside her car, a window open, our clothes everywhere. My mind was travelling, travelling without moving, while S- looked as if she was about to fall asleep while holding her cigarette mid-air. I saw the smoke go up, circle around the car, slowly vanish or escape through the little gaps in the car windows. And while I was there with S- I thought of Achy, another woman I used to love, and I wondered how she was, where she was, was she loving someone else, and I felt sad, not sad for the fact that Achy might be loving someone else but sad for the fact I had her and let her go.

(I read —and reread- what I wrote so many years ago, this while living in Portugal. I read —and reread- and some of it I keep and some I don't. Some memories are shredded and later forgotten.)

-I don't think I'll ever see S- or Achy again. Then again, knowing how unpredictable life can be, who knows?

I told S- that maybe we should put some clothes on, just in case some cops drove past and saw us there, and she laughed and said, "Have you seen where we are? I don't think the police will come here."

"Maybe you're right but what if you're wrong?" I said.

She puffed and huffed and stayed where she was, her body on full display, same as mine, but as I looked at her naked body I felt nothing. I was too tired, too drained to feel a thing.

My body was satisfied, completely full, as if I had been fasting for a long period of time and then was fed by S-. And as I sat here with her, contemplating the darkness around us, I found myself thinking about the time I spent in London with Achy, and I realised that I missed London more than I missed Achy. But I also missed Achy, and given the choice between Achy and London or S- and Portimão, I would have chosen London and Achy. (But lately I've been missing Portimão but not London.)

S- finally went over to the front seat and put on some clothes. I finished my cigarette before putting on some clothes too.

Afterwards S- drove us to Praia do Vau where we saw a couple of familiar cars parked close to the beach. Our friends Telma, Sandro, Caio and Elsa were also out and about, smoking crap, hallucinating, travelling without moving, enjoying the silence, the humidity, an almost abandoned beach.

No one was surprised to see anyone. In Portimão you would leave your home, walk somewhere, and most of the time you were bound to bump into a friend. (This is one of the reasons why I miss Portimão.)

Caio and Sandro were sitting on the sand, sharing a joint while the women were talking close to the sea, their feet on the water. S- went over to chat with the women while I sat next to Sandro.

"Want some?" Caio asked as he put the joint close to my face. I nodded no.

"I've already smoked too much with S-," I said.

Caio shrugged his shoulders and passed the joint to Sandro.

We could hear the women talking and laughing.

I felt at ease on the beach, close to the sea. I wish I could live there, have a small apartment overlooking the sea, share my apartment with a good woman, have a desk by one of the windows so that, in the mornings, I could sit down to write.

"Maybe one day," I told myself. (But I don't think that day will come, not in Portimão. Maybe I'll have my apartment –and desk- somewhere else.)

A few minutes gone past, we saw a police car on the distant horizon, slowly approaching. I exchanged looks with the lads but neither of us said a word. As for the women, they kept on talking. And laughing. Really loud.

Caio and Sandro reached for their cigarettes, and I asked Sandro for a cigarette. He smoked red Ducados while Caio smoked SG Gigante, a brand that I never liked. The cigarettes calmed us down and we made our best to ignore the cops who by now were driving past our cars, probably looking out of the windows, looking to see if we were doing anything illegal. The women must have seen the police car too but they kept on talking. And they laughed so loud.

"Bloody women," Caio said. "Can they be any louder?"

The cops left shortly afterwards. Sandro looked tired. Actually, he looked bored. He had only recently returned from Germany and he told us he was thinking of going back (to Germany); go back and settle there, get a job with his cousin; his cousin Eduardo was working in Hamburg as a cook. (He's still there, in Germany, in Berlin, I heard from someone, still working as a cook.)

"Life is good there. The city is…" Sandro looked lost, as if he was searching for the right word.

The women were still talking. And laughing.

What was there to talk about for so long? And why the laughter?

"Bleak. No! Wait. Dark. Darker than Portimão. Darker than any city I've been to in Portugal," Sandro said. "You wake up in the morning and the sky is grey. You go to work and the sky is grey, like dark grey. You leave work and the sky is dark. But there's life in Germany, a different type of life; life and mystery."

He told us of a party he went to in Hamburg where he and a bunch of people listened to classical music throughout the night.

"Nothing but Schubert, Liszt and Brahms throughout the night," Sandro said, and then smiled as he relived that night. "The opposite of a rave, when you think about it, but it was so peaceful, you know?"

I nodded. As for Caio, he looked as if he was about to fall asleep right there on the spot.

"People spoke, you know. People actually spoke. Mostly about art. Literature. Now that I think about it, you would have loved it, M÷," Sandro said. And I nodded, again.

"This woman named Ilse —what a beautiful name; and she, too, was gorgeous, a blonde goddess with big blue eyes- told me a story about Heinrich Heine. She probably told me the whole life story of Heine, and I didn't even know who the hell Heinrich Heine was. But I wrote his name down. Actually, she was the one who wrote it down for me. And as I sat there listening to her, and listening to the music, I felt as if I had travelled back in time; gone back to a different era, an era where people listened to music without having the need to jump around and shout and swear, an era where music was actually enjoyable and where people talked about literature and art and life and even damn politics. And sometime throughout the night I saw that maybe I needed a change of airs, maybe settle down in Germany for a long time, read and learn German, listen to Schubert and Schumann and Liszt and all those German classical composers for the rest of my life and…"

Caio interrupted Sandro and said, "Actually, Schubert was from Austria."

"What?" Sandro shot back.

"He's right. And Liszt was Hungarian," I said.

And then, for some strange reason, the three of us laughed even louder than the women.

(Sandro never went back to Germany. Last I've heard of him, he was still living in Portimão.)

Psalm 9:13

Women aren't the enemy of Men, just as Men aren't the Enemy of Women. We must learn to love one another, regardless of gender, race or religion. After all, aren't we all the same?

I could love Alice Walker just as I could love Michelle Yeoh just as I could love Patti Smith just as I could love Kim Wilde just as I could love Oprah Winfrey.

A cold morning. I close the notebook and put it in the inside pocket of my black coat. An empty cup of coffee in front of me. Nowhere to go, no one to see. What an empty life.

I found a loose sheet of paper inside one of my notebooks. Undated. Written in London during the 90s.

25th September 2015

Yu is quick to criticise (and shout) but never to praise. As a matter of fact, she never praises me, hardly ever says a kind word. I'm not even allowed to comment on her Facebook page. If I do such a thing she'll get mad with me but says nothing when her friends comment on her idiotic Facebook page.

Sometimes, sometimes…

Sometimes I wonder if I did a mistake by marrying her too quickly.

Sometimes I wonder if she (still?) loves me.

And has she ever loved me?

I think she only loves herself.

She wants and wants and wants but she can never give.

(I read what I wrote so many years ago and, again, come to the conclusion that Yu never ever loved me. Her family were right about her. She's too selfish, too cold.)

There's poetry in sadness. Sadly, I can't write a word of it.

May 31st, 2021

Three days without seeing my children.

Three days of longing, three long days, long days of sadness.

Three days of despair, days of darkness.

Some days I don't want to live.

This life I'm living right now is no life.

This is death. A slow, painful death.

This afternoon (I died, again)…

This afternoon I looked at a wall and saw nothing.

I looked and saw nothing and no one.

I saw nothing and no one waiting for me.

Nothing and no one.

This afternoon I went for a walk, and loneliness and sadness kept me company. And when I cried, they both clapped hands.

This afternoon…

This afternoon loneliness paid me a visit.

And last afternoon, too.

And the afternoon before that.

And…

This afternoon Yu took our children to a barbeque at the house of one of her religious friends. Yu is very religious, yes, she is. She worships the Snake. Her first commandment is gimme, gimme, gimme. The second commandment is, "If you can't give me nothing, goodbye."

I cry inside when I think of my children far away from me, living a life without me, a life where I'm a ghost-like figure.

I cry, and sometimes I die; I die, just a tiny bit, but Yu can't know of my pain. In the past, when I told her of my depression, she made fun of it, fun of me, so now I hide it, from her, from everyone.

I cry, to myself only, when I'm walking, when I'm sitting in the park, on a bench, outside a church. I cry but I hide it.

G-d willing, one day the pain will leave me, and maybe my children will be with me. And those who hurt me might get a tiny taste of my pain. But I hope they don't.

It saddens me when I think of my children so far away from me, enjoying a barbeque with others, without me. It saddens me because I will miss so much; their laughter, a joke from my daughter, a comment from my son, and what I'm losing now I will never be able to get back. And while they're living a life away from me, I head to the city centre for a walk. I buy a sandwich and a bottle of juice from Tesco, the cheapest sandwich I can get from Tesco, and then I sit on a park, alone, eating, crying, drinking juice and tears, dying bit by bit. But my mind keeps showing me glimpses of something else, glimpses of a New Life, glimpses that turn into Hope.

I shake the Sadness away.

I must live.

I must live on.

Scary days ahead. The news keeps on selling fear, warning us of another possible lockdown, telling us that without a vaccine we won't be able to keep our jobs. That's bad news for me because I don't want a vaccine against the Invisible Enemy. A lot of people that I know have taken the vaccine but a few others, like me, Saul, my friend Paula and her husband Emmanuel have refused it.

Yu always said she wouldn't take it but she finally gave in a couple of weeks ago. My friend and colleague Olly also said he would never take the vaccine, no matter what, and he came up with some crazy theories about the vaccine (but what if he was right?), but he has an appointment to take it this week. And from what Olly told me, our colleague Patrick has already taken the first vaccine.

For the last few months Olly has been saying, "I won't take the vaccine, no matter what. I don't know what's in there." But now he has changed his mind about it. And today he was saying to me, "If you don't take the vaccine, you won't be able to work"

I shrugged my shoulders and said, "Then I won't work."

"How will you live?" Olly asked.

"I won't," I said. "I might move into a tent and then slowly vanish away, disintegrate into the atmosphere, go up in the air, join the cosmos."

He said nothing.

I've noticed that Olly has picked up a few habits from Patrick. He even copies the other man's speech. Seeing that Patrick isn't the smartest cat on the block (and his speech is quite rude), that's not a smart move.

Only a few months ago Olly was acting so defiant when it came to the Invisible Enemy and its vaccines (for now you have to take two vaccines; later, who knows?) but now he looks resigned to his faith.

I look around me, at the state of the world, and I see that we're heading towards the total collapse of society. A wide prison is being built around us, built by chaos and division, and a lot of people seem oblivious to it. The "changes" are already here, but the ones in power want to force more changes on us. And with the help of the media, which they control, they're achieving just that. Scary days ahead but I've been talking about this for years.

I've seen the changes from afar.

For a while, when I was a bit lost; brainwashed by the Lies around me, I accepted those changes, but with the help of Christ, and my renewed faith on the Lord (but how strong is my faith?), I saw that some of those changes are wrong.

The Invisible Hand that controls the world is telling the people to mutilate the Temple (the Body) and that everything will be OK, but how can it be OK to destroy G-d's Creation?

I read somewhere that solar storms are back and that they can become a threat to life on Earth. Later I also read that the SEG Plaza in Shenzhen, China began to shake for no apparent reason and that people fled in panic from the skyscraper. There were no reports of an earthquake in the region and no one knows what to make of it. Strange days we're living through, yes.

Meanwhile, in Congo, a deadly volcano has erupted, no warning whatsoever. And a few days ago, on May 22nd, in China's Qinghai Province, a magnitude − 7.4 earthquake woke up everyone a few minutes after 2AM. For the last few days China has been hit by a few earthquakes.

What's happening around the world?

Meanwhile, on Facebook, some friends of mine are adding profile photos saying that they had the jab against the Invisible Enemy. They feel compelled to share that piece of information with the world, as if it was a badge of honour, but why? Some of them no longer speak to me but why?

Even my friend Santiago is distancing himself from me. A few days ago, an hour or two before Shabbos was about to start, I texted him on Signal to wish him a Gut Shabbos, and he texted me back, saying that we must meet soon, and I said, "Sure. That sounds good. How about next month?"

Santiago said, "Next month sounds good. Have you had your vaccines? Both vaccines?"

I told him I refused to have any vaccine and that I don't intend to have any. I haven't heard from him ever since then.

A few other people at the reform shul that I used to attend also stopped talking to me but why?

Strange days are coming our way, days of hunger, anger, snitching; the former agents of PIDE and Stasi are laughing; days of no morals, days when right will be wrong and wrong will be the law. Scary days, I tell you.

Days of loneliness.

Days of no love.

Days of hate.

Months of hate.

Years of hate?

The media will keep on selling fear. It already has a new Agenda on the way; the Eco-Agenda: more fear to sell, sponsored by the Invisible Hand. Your favourite rock star and movie star and whoever have sold their souls to the Dark Prince and they will front this Agenda and tell you how to live your lives. No travelling for you. Meanwhile those behind the Eco-Agenda will travel the world on their private jets. It's a joke, and the joke's on you.

There will be more shouting, more barking (the woke generation tends to bark at those who disagree with them), and a lot of snitching. And let's not forget the tears. There will be tears too, lots of them, and blood; lots of it, rivers of blood. Say a prayer, save your soul. By the way, Duran Duran are back with a new single. You got to laugh a bit, laugh before they get you, and afterwards pray for a quick end.

Will I see that unvaccinated pretty blonde, blue-eyed, yellowed-teeth woman soon?

I see no poetry in pain, no poetry in sadness, but there's a lot of it to be found there. The problem is I'm not a poet.

A week ago I dreamt that Yu was going out with another man, and this morning I found out that she actually went out with another man last week, probably on the same day that I had the dream, and she took our children with them. This man drove them to Leicester, took them to McDonald's, and then they went shopping. How nice. I also found out that this man's name is Colin, his arms are full of tattoos (I thought Yu hated tattoos), he only has one leg, and that's about it. To be honest, I don't care if Yu has a new man or not.

Going back and forth through some of my old notes, I see (read) that our marriage died ages ago. Years ago.

September 17th, 2015

An argument this morning, straight out of the blue, followed by a screaming contest. Yu easily won the contest as I can't be bothered to scream. Okay, I admit it; I did a mistake, but it was an accident, a minor accident (but perfect Yu Li won't even accept minor mistakes). What happened was I put the clothes on the dryer, making sure to leave some of them hanging but only the ones that can shrink on the dryer. Unfortunately I didn't notice one of Yu's skirts on the pile of clothes that I put on the dryer. And so, the skirt shrunk, just a tiny bit (or so Yu said but for all I know she could just be looking for an excuse to shout at me because she loves the shouting), and I apologised for it at least ten times (actually, it was more than ten times), but Yu ignored my apologies and kept on shouting and shouting, and when I went a bit sad she even laughed about it and said, "Oh, you are depressed now. Poor you."

She mocked me a bit more and pretended to be wiping invisible tears from her eyes.

Yu's a vile creature. She reminds me of Grandmother at her worse.

Yu did some minor work on the skirt and it fits her fine, but she's still upset with me, and she will shout if I say anything. How can I stay married to a woman who doesn't even accept an apology?

Even though I'm tired, and feeling a bit poorly; maybe I'm coming down with a cold, I still went out for a walk with my daughter. It's better than staying at home staring at Yu's cold face. With her everything always starts and ends with an argument and shouting. I'm too tired to argue and I'm not good at shouting. Yu says she's nothing like my grandmother but they're so alike.

What have I done?

I married a stone.

A stone can't love.

A stone doesn't know what love is.

Leaf and I play football at the park and afterwards we feed the squirrels. While we're in town I bump into my friend Cassio whom I haven't seen in a long time. So far, Cassio's my only Portuguese friend in Coventry. He tells me he started attending a Catholic church near his home and we promised to meet more often. From there I quickly head to the library with my daughter. I get a book by Jenny Erpenbeck called *The End of Days*, and then it's time to go home. And face the noise. Or the silence and ignorance.

Reading these words that I wrote years ago no longer upset me, and I'm not even going to spend my time hating Yu. She is who she is (and she's getting worse with age), and someone else can put up with her.

3rd June 2021

The name Colin sounded familiar and I realised that Yu is dating someone from the firm we work for. From what the children told me, Colin comes to stay at Yu's place almost every night, probably after I've gone home. Yu's smart; she wants me at her place on the daytime to look after the kids and at night she has Colin with her. But isn't Colin married?

Yesterday, and the day before, when she got home from work Yu looked really guilty, so guilty that she couldn't even look me in the eye, and I didn't even bother to say much to her.

A few minutes before I went home, Yu got a call from someone from her church, and afterwards Yu started to badmouth someone called Trish, saying that Trish said that Yu always needs favours and always wants people to do things for her, which is true (and this Trish has done a lot of favours to Yu, but her kids aren't that nice towards Leaf and, if alone with my daughter, they tend to bully Leaf), and I saw were the conversation (and Yu's life) was heading. Sooner or later she'll stop being friends with this Trish because if she can no longer get anything from her friend Yu will cut her out of her life without giving it a second thought. And then I thought of this Colin with Yu. I know that he earns well and has a bit of money. Is that the reason why Yu's going out with him?

Yu's life a comedy waiting to become a tragedy. As for mine, it's already a tragedy and I must find a way out; a path to happiness.

I found it all so laughable; Mormon Yu going out with (married?) atheist Colin. I even found a hidden containment of coffee in her kitchen. Mormon Yu always hated when I drank coffee (ironically, I have now cut down on my caffeine intake) and now her new (married?) man drinks coffee. Yes, a comedy turning into a tragedy. But I don't want to play a role in that Divine Comedy. I have my own *À la reserche du tems perdu* to write. Actually, now that I think about it, I should write something along the lines of *La Nausée* instead. I'm already becoming some sort of Roquentin. But I still care... for some people.

Later I find out that Colin is actually divorced.

Sorrow...

I feel sorrow for Yu (but I must be selfish and think of me first); sorrow because, unless she changes her ways, one day she'll be alone. At times she looks like the character of Sylvia from Leonard Michael's novel *Sylvia*. And that's all there is to say.

A tragedy waiting to happen.

I forgot to mention that this Colin dude is a smoker, and Yu always said she would never date a smoker.

A tragedy...

Then again, she also said that she would never date a non-Mormon. Or a guy with tattoos. Hmm, a certain name comes to mind when I think of her.

Forgive and flee

7th October 2015

Last night, everything was okay.

No fighting, no shouting, no arguing.

Unfortunately it won't last

And what am I doing here?

Living with this cold woman?

We spoke for a long time, the longest we've spoken in ages (but the only reason why we spoke for so long is because she has a problem, and when Yu has a problem she wants me to stop whatever I'm doing and listen to her, but if the roles were reversed she would say that I moan a lot), and Yu told me she needs to go back to church, go back to Christ, back to the Lord, but not the Mormon church. She told me she needs a change, get closer to G-d, to be around normal people and not self-proclaimed righteous people. I know how she feels. That's why I left.

June 2021. I read what I wrote so many years ago. And then I go back even further, to the years 2009 and 2010. My marriage to Yu Li was a disaster, but, nonetheless, I always stayed by her side and played the role of faithful husband to perfection. Was I an idiot for having done such a thing? No, of course not. I don't regret that. The truth is I never wanted to be a ladies' man and fool around with various women. As naïve as this may sound, I always wanted to have one person to love, one woman only, and have my home and my family, and that's it. My father did a lot of fooling around, slept with various women, was never faithful to any of his wives, but that's not the type of life that I want to live. I want a quiet life, a good woman by my side, a woman with whom I can discuss the works of Plato, Hustvedt, Sartre, and even

Oprah in one breath. I think my ideal woman would be someone like Patti Smith. I've read and reread *M Train* and *The Year of the Monkey* countless of times, and I felt as if I was reading my own words or reading my own thoughts. Or something like that.

Patti reads the writers and poets that I like, and we kind of like some of the same foods, not to mention we both love coffee, although lately I've cut down on the caffeine quite drastically, and I go entire days without drinking coffee. Due to health issues I've changed my diet and had to reduce my caffeine intake. Ever since I've stopped drinking coffee in huge quantities, I've noticed that my head feels lighter, as if I'm wearing an invisible hat. The first two days without coffee were quite strange, not to mention a bit difficult, and that's when my head felt a bit strange, as if I was wearing a cold invisible hat on my head, but then I got used to it, to that lifestyle, and the tremors on my forehead stopped, which only shows that I needed a change in my lifestyle. I still drink coffee, a cup every two days, sometimes a cup every three days, but I can see myself reducing it even more. I used to drink four cups of coffee a day, and my eating habits weren't that healthy either, so, like I've said (or wrote), I do needed a change in my lifestyle. Some nights, when I'm at work, I drink a Huel shake instead of getting an unhealthy takeaway meal. I've also gone back to meditating; I had stopped for a while but I need to regain both my physical and my mental health. Anyway, going back to Patti. I could see myself living with a woman like her; a quiet soul, a poetic woman, a woman that, even on the way she dresses, looks a bit like me.

Saturday, 5ᵗʰ June 2021. A day of dark thoughts (and here I was talking about a new lifestyle), tears, wanting to die. I slept for a few hours in the morning, then went to Bell Green, to Cassio's place. I bought a cooked chicken for us from Sainsbury's. When I got to Cassio's place, he wasn't yet at home so I went to a café called Luxury Bakery, a small cafeteria run by two ladies. There was a couple inside the cafeteria having a full breakfast. Their plates were full of food; beans, eggs, sausages, bacon, toast, tomatoes; way too much food. I ordered a cup of coffee and sat outside where I wrote and waited for Cassio to arrive. He arrived an hour later. Already he'd been gambling. And he lost. Later, he had to go to town and pawn his mobile phone. He's always doing that. Anyway, after lunch at Cassio's place, we went back to town, back to the city centre (because Cassio had to pawn his phone, and after he left the shop I could see him looking at the gambling house), and from there we went our separate ways. I spent almost three hours in town doing nothing, looking at a book and not reading, looking around me and seeing nothing but emptiness and darkness inside me. While I was there, alone, staring at nothingness and darkness, Yu was enjoying her new life, a life of taking, taking, taking, and never giving. I missed my children so badly. I missed their smiles, having them around me, and I knew that it would be a long time before I could have my own place so that I could spend more time with them. I thought that, with time, life would get easier, but, so far, that hasn't been the case. If anything, life is getting easier for Yu.

My heart felt heavy, dark, broken, and I felt so tired, really tired, as if I had nothing to live for, as if I could not make it through another day, as if time was running out for me and the only thing left for me to do was…die? Wait? Wait for death?

Wait…

Wednesday, 9th June 2021. On Monday I had to make a strong effort to go to work. I stood on Little Park Street for a few minutes, wondering where to go. I wanted to head somewhere else, not to work, disappear for a long time, live on the streets for a long time, see no one that I know for a long time, quit, give up, die. Life without my children was becoming almost unbearable, but how many parents haven't gone through what I'm going through?

I went deep inside myself searching for strength, for hope, for that "bit" that connects me to the Creator. I found something, I think, a connection to the Creator, to the Universe, and so I moved forward. (On Monday) it was another lonely night at work but at least I spent a few hours with my daughter in the afternoon. Too bad I didn't get to see my son as he was still at school.

Four days without seeing my son. Three days without seeing my daughter. No wonder I was feeling a bit low. But there's a bit of light ahead, a bit of hope on the horizon, and I can't give up, not yet, not ever. I must dig deep inside myself and find (in me) the strength to carry on even though there are times when I want to quit. But quitting means dying.

Cassio called me. He needs money. He always needs money.

He spends the little he earns gambling and afterwards he sells a few things that he has or he borrows money from me and a few others. Not so long ago he bought a brand-new laptop for more than £300 pounds, and a few weeks later he sold it for £150 pounds. Gold chains, gold rings, £300 pounds mobile phones, expensive watches; you name it, he bought it for a lot of money and then sold it for a bargain because he spent the rest of his money gambling. He even admitted to me more than once that he could have bought a house long ago if he didn't gamble.

This time I couldn't help him. I told him so. I have some money saved for rainy days and I'm saving a bit more to buy a car, and I can't be lending money to Cassio almost every two weeks. He just doesn't learn. And he still owes me money.

His brother committed suicide because of gambling. Cassio himself is going a bit crazy, and sometimes he shouts at his TV because he thinks that the people on TV are making fun of him. Crazy, yes.

I need a change of life, new friends, normal friends, but nowadays normal seems to be a rarity.

From what my son told me, the romance between Colin and Yu seems to have ended. She even told our children to ignore Colin if they ever see him. I wonder what happened. But do I even care? I used to but now, I don't know. I don't think I do. Actually, I don't.

A few things happened in the last few days. There's a bit of light ahead, a bit of hope, and I'm starting to forget Yu.

Forget You.

A lot of talk online about the Invisible Enemy. The virus is mutating, getting stronger, and it looks as if it will stay with us for a long time, but I already knew this and I told a lot of my friends about it.

"It could be a weapon. In fact, I believe that it is one," Saul says. "A weapon created by the Chinese government, a bio-weapon that will exterminate a lot of us."

I don't know what to say.

What if he's right?

Almost everyone that I know has been vaccinated but do the vaccines even work against the Invisible Enemy? In other news, a few billionaires want to travel to the moon, maybe to another planet. Maybe they want to leave us behind. But then what will they do in another planet? They will get fat. And die. Not much difference from life on Earth. But maybe they know something else that we don't. Maybe they know that the ending is coming, that the ending is imminent, and that it will arrive from space. Maybe...

"Are you Left or Right?" Saul asked.

"No," I replied.

I want a little house somewhere, in a quiet area. A bit of land so I can grow my own food. My children with me. Good books to read. A good woman by my side. I want a lot, yes, all that I don't have.

I finally got an allotment. Actually, my friend Emma's the one who's renting it, but she told me she needed some help with it and that I could grow my own food there so I said yes straight away. I've known Emma for the last 18 months but I didn't see her for almost a year. But now I've finally decided to start living, forget the past (but how many times haven't I said that in the last few months?), forget the past and the lies, the pain, the evil eye, and just move on. I'm writing a bit more, working on different projects, finally typing my novel *The Invisible Hand*, meeting new people, going out for a bit, etc.

Last week me and Emma spent an entire afternoon working in the allotment. My children were with us for a couple of hours and Yu picked them up before 6PM. Seeing her now does nothing to me. I don't even want her as a friend. Social distancing; that's what I want from her. 200 miles apart, not 2 meters. One way or another, she'll always feature in my life, hopefully as a minor character, but these are still early days and we have children in common, a long past together, but that's what she is; the past, a painful reminder of the past.

Yu met Emma, they chatted for a while, and a few minutes later Yu and the children left. I hardly looked at her. Nowadays, whenever I see her, I hardly look at her. She's a face that I no longer like, a face that I find to be quite ugly. Looking at her now I can't even believe that I actually got married to her. She deceived me with that body, with that tongue, with lies and fake smiles. But she must have loved me a bit. It couldn't all just been a lie, could it?

After Yu and the children were gone, me and Emma stayed for a bit longer at the allotment. There was a lot of work to be done there and we did as much as we could, but we couldn't do it all in one afternoon and we would have to return a few days later. From there we went to McDonald's for something to eat and a long chat.

I found out that Emma was a really caring person, someone who was also hurt by life and the selfish actions of others, and I enjoyed spending time with her.

On that same afternoon, on my way home, I bumped into a couple that I know by Mount Street. Their names are Cassandra and Gary, and I've kind of known Cassandra for longer than a year now. In fact, when I first met her, I was still living in Carlton Court with the children and Yu, and I used to bump into Cassandra quite often on the way from school with Leaf. Not so long ago, Cassandra introduced me to her husband Gary. I liked him straight away. He seems to be a quiet person, a bit like me, genuine. On that same afternoon I spoke a bit longer with them and I found out, from both Cassandra and Gary, that Gary also went through a bad phase after his divorce, but, like he said, "Life goes on, and better things will come your way."

I hope he's right.

I told them both how, after my divorce (and after being told repeatedly that I'm too good), I wanted to be a bit colder, even cruel, but Cassandra said, "No. Don't. Be yourself and you will see that, in the end, everything will turn out to be for the best."

Gary nodded and said, "I went through the same. Just be yourself. And give it time."

Give Time to Life to be kind(er) to you.

Reading the works of poet Kim Min Jeong. Father's Day. No one calls me. No one texts me. Oh well, life goes on.

Tuesday, June 22nd. A relaxing day, just the kind of day I needed. After work I went straight home, got into bed a few minutes after 7AM. This morning, as I sometimes do, I slept on my sleeping bag. There's a large bed in my bedroom but, every once in a while, I like to sleep in the sleeping bag. Headphones on, I fell asleep to the voice of Kelly Howell. I've been listening to her for the last couple of years. I'm in love with her voice. The house was silent. In the room next door, Liz was also sleeping.

I got up a few minutes after 11AM, showered, ate something, said a few prayers, replied to some messages on WhatsApp, then went out. A dark sky greeted me when I stepped out of the house. The weather was a mixture of cold and hot, as if it couldn't decide what to be. I took a jumper with me, just in case, took the 6A bus to the city centre, and then made my way to the Coventry Jesus Centre. It wasn't yet 1PM. The Centre would open its doors at 1PM for coffee and lunch. My friend Julian was already waiting outside. We met a few months ago, at a food bank near Pool Meadow Bus Station. Julian lives on the streets, sleeps wherever he can, eats whatever he can. He's 55-years old, has no kids, got sick of working non-stop, working on factories, working on meaningless jobs, so he took a break from it all. Can't say I blame him for it. It's not the type of life I would have chosen for myself but people are different.

I'm trying to get a council flat, a place I can call home. It would be great if I could buy my own home, but, at the moment, that's not possible; maybe I will never be able to buy my own place; Yu was lucky; she got some inheritance money, took it all, and told me to go screw myself. Anyway, if I could get a council flat, I would refurbish it my way, make it a good home for rest, a place where I could escape the outside world, and get my own meditation corner. Only time will tell what will happen.

Going back to Julian; like me, he also doesn't believe half the stuff he hears on the news.

We sat outside for a bit, talking about life, the world, the meaningless of it all, the meaningless of hate and greed and jealousy. There were other men waiting outside, people from all parts of the world. Different races, different religions, atheists, all together in one place, in a house of G-d, a house of Christ, eating, playing snooker, drinking coffee and tea, etc., and no arguments.

Me and Julian spoke about the Invisible Enemy and the Invisible Hand, and how the world is going through a drastic change, and he mentioned how someone came with the slogan, "No Jab, No Job", a scary slogan, the jab in reference to the Invisible Enemy's vaccine, a vaccine that some people say is the Mark of the Beast, and, if later, the Invisible Hand decides that those who haven't taken the jab won't be able to work, I'll be in big trouble because I've decided long ago not to take the jab. Julian too has said no to the jab.

The media, owned by the Invisible Hand, keep on selling fear, day after day, constantly selling fear and telling people to get vaccinated. I told Julian that the Invisible Hand (and the media) keep on creating division amongst the people because, that way, they can control us better, and this new generation, the so-called woke generation (but there's a lot of goodness in this new generation, a lot of good hearts, people that just need to find themselves), the snowflake generation (but I'm one of them, too), are so fragile, weak, and sensitive that they can't see a thing apart from what they read and/or see on the news. They are being brainwashed, being told to "transform" themselves, destroy themselves, abort, abort at all costs, destroy G-d's creation, and they're okay with it.

Julian agreed with what I was saying and he also mentioned the fact that some people want to banish the Greek classics (and other classic works of literature...Dostoevsky? Chekhov? Proust?) because they're too white, or whatever, and even though I couldn't believe what I was hearing, I wasn't surprised by it. Not so long ago I read how a couple of writers had to change and edit a couple of books that they had recently published for the simple fact that they were hurting the feelings of some people. Really? Maybe I was right and the writer is dead...

We're living in an age where we can't even call a man a man and a woman a woman lest we hurt the feelings of some people. Madness. Yes, we've reached the age of madness. Soon we won't be able to call madness madness just in case we hurt someone. What a farce. This is why I need my own place, a little corner where I can escape society. And the madness.

After I left the Jesus Centre, I saw a young man sitting nearby. He was smoking a roll up and I could tell he needed a meal. I almost walked past him but for some reason I decided to go over to where he was and say hello to him and tell him that he could get something to eat from the Jesus Centre. He was sitting on the grass and he greeted me back, and after I mentioned the Jesus Centre and that he could get something to eat from there, he asked me if I worked for the Jesus Centre and I said no, adding that I worked as a security guard, at a nearby building. He then asked me my name and I told him I was M÷. He said, "My name is Francis..." and he mentioned a few other names before adding, "I'm Jesus. The real Jesus. I've just been released from prison. By the way, what's happening in the world?"

I didn't know what to say but I told him about the Invisible Enemy, the madness around us, and Francis (probably not his real name) said, "I hear voices in the air. Artificial Intelligence. The world is going through a change. A new beginning will soon be upon us."

I didn't know what to say.

In the end, I told him one more time to go to the Jesus Centre and get something to eat.

Before I left, Francis shook my hand, and then he gave me a hug. He wished me luck and told me to take care. I nodded and said, "You take care too."

I sure meet some strange people this year.

From there I went straight to the bus stop, took the 11 bus to Earlsdon, read a few pages of *All The Light We Cannot See*, which Cassandra lent me, and then I picked up my daughter from school. I've mentioned this before but I don't spend enough time with my children. A few minutes here and there every few days is not enough but what can I do? For now, this is the best I can get. If I think too much about I'll end up crying. And then the bad thoughts will return.

I took Leaf back to her mother's place. Matthew was already home, glued to his laptop. Every time I go to Yu's place Matthew's always glued to the laptop. If it's not the laptop it's the mobile phone. He doesn't want to be away from any of those devices. If he could he would never leave home. He would just stay glued to his laptop. There are days when I feel like doing the same. But my son does read a lot, too, so maybe I'm being a bit unfair. But he does spend a lot of time glued to his laptop.

At Yu's place I watch a few clips of YouTubers Remainings and Citizen with Leaf. She likes Citizen but I prefer Remainings. Citizen and Remainings are Roblox gamers who also have their own YouTube channels. I've got my own YouTube channel too, which I've started just for fun, dedicated mostly to unknown myth games on Roblox. I like to play obscure games, or games that aren't well known to the public, and, sometimes, I record clips of those games and post it on YouTube. I've got some followers, and some of them appreciate the fact that I play lesser known games. My daughter tends to play Meep City, and similar games, while I tend to play what gamers call myth hunts.

Yu arrived home a few minutes before 6PM. The moment she was in through the front door I got ready to leave, but she asked me to stay for a bit longer and spend some time with the children. I stayed in the living room with Leaf while Matthew never left his bedroom. As for Yu, she cooked dinner. A few minutes later the three of them sat down to eat while I sat there staring at nothing. Leaf was crying, complaining about dinner, as she often does, making excuses not to eat, and I was tired and hungry (I'd only slept three hours, if that, and my body was ready to shut down), but Yu doesn't seem to understand that others also need to rest. She wants to come home and have everyone running after her, doing things for her, but she forgets that people also need.

I read something a few days ago that read something like, forgive and forget but don't have amnesia, but, no matter how hard I try, as of yet, I can't forgive and forget Yu's betrayal. She left me with nothing at a time when the world was in lockdown, and if it hadn't been for me, she would have almost nothing, not even a job, but she's so greedy and selfish that she can't even see that. That's why I can't forgive or forget what she did to me. One day, G-d willing, I will have my own place, a good woman by my side, my children staying with me more often, and I will have almost nothing to do with Yu. And later, much later, I would like to move as further away from her as possible and never see her again. It will happen, and maybe then she will realise what a good man I was and that I truly loved her.

I watched Yu sat her fat arse on her new sofa, a big plate of food in front of her ugly face. Meanwhile Leaf kept on crying. Matthew was still glued to his laptop, a plate of food in front of him, and my tired hungry body said, "Go home, man. Look after yourself too."

And so I got up and told Yu I had to go. I want to spend as much time as I can with my children, but I also need to look after myself. Not so long ago I ended up in hospital because of high blood pressure, but thanks to a good diet I've managed to get back to normal, and I don't want to go through that again. But Yu doesn't care what happens to me or others just as long as she's okay. If I was to say that to her; that she's selfish and cold and even cruel, she would deny it and then she would come up with some lame excuse, mention things that never happened, things that only happened in her crazy head, say that I did this or that, but the truth is she pushes everyone away and that's why she has lost touch with every single member of her family and all of her old friends. Still, she can't see her wrongdoings. And then she gets jealous of the fact that I'm still in touch with most of my old friends from Portugal. What a bitch. Yes, forgive and forget. Just don't get amnesia and forget what a cruel bitch Yu was (and is).

I went home, ate something, typed for a bit (a hate story for you, Yu), then sat in bed, lights off, thinking of my children. A few tears escaped my eyes.

"I don't want to be here," I thought.

But where can I go?

For now, I must wait.

But wait for what?

And for how long?

Wednesday, 23rd June 2021

I was thinking, "What if I killed myself? What would happen to my notebooks and all those unpublished stories and novels that I wrote?"

The darkness is always there, ever present in my life, along with the sadness, a remainder that I'm not there yet, out of the darkness.

Love died and left me alone in the dark.

Now what?

Now I move on, forward, sometimes slowly, sometimes at a steady pace.

I saw my daughter this morning for less than ten minutes. I waited outside her school, waited for her mother to drop her at school, waited for a glimpse of happiness, a way out of the darkness. This is my life now; a few minutes here and there with my children, if I'm lucky enough to get that. And selfish cow, cruel snake, fat bitch Yu wonders why I'm sad. I can't forgive or forget, not unless I get amnesia.

After dropping Leaf at school, I took the 11 bus to the city centre. I went to Starbucks in 52 Broadgate, ordered a filter coffee (my first and only cup of the day), and then sat down and wrote a few entries on my journal, including this, and while I was at the café I saw Francis walk past. He didn't see me.

He was wearing the same clothes as yesterday, and he was carrying a large rucksack. He came inside Starbucks, only to use the bathroom, and he was in there for quite a long time. I watched him leave the café, head down, another lost soul in the world.

Nothing to do, nowhere to go, no one to see.

It would be good to have someone by my side, a new woman in my life, a good woman, not a bitch, a bit of loving.

Love dies and it takes more than three days for it to resurrect.

I can see why Uncle J gave up on our family. He probably spent decades crying, missing those he loved/loves, working hard, working long hours, living a lonely life, only to see that, in the end, those he missed and loved only cared about money, and so he chose to forget everyone and just live a quiet life with those who really care about him. Uncle J retired and moved back to Portugal but he lives far away from our family because he knows that some people only want his money. He used to send money to Grandmother, a lot of money, and she probably gave some of it, if not most of it, to my brother Carlos, but they forget that Uncle J also needs to live. And why should he be giving them money all the time?

People are so selfish, so greedy. I can see why Uncle J gave up the family. Maybe one day I'll do the same.

I went to Central Library, cried for a bit in there, took out two books; *The Dinner Guest* by Gabriela Ybarra and *The Lost Pianos of Siberia* by Sophy Roberts, and afterwards I sat outside the Jesus Centre and read for a bit. But before I read, I cried.

I need to stop crying.

No one's crying for me so why am I wasting my tears?

Part of me wants to die.

Part of me wants to live a long life so that I can see my children grow and be there for them when/if they need me.

Maybe Cassandra was wrong.

Maybe I need to become a bit colder.

Not enough people care.

Why should I care?

But is that the way to live?

The reason why the world is in such a mess is because not enough people care.

Maybe Cassandra is right.

Maybe I shouldn't become cold.

After all, the world needs a bit of warmness.

Not so long ago I joined a dating site. A few days later I saw that Brie had also joined that same dating site. I quickly closed my account. Brie was the last woman I went out with after my relationship with Yu came to an end, but even though she's a lovely person, she just didn't feel right. Maybe it was too soon for me to move on. And now I want to move on but I need a fresher face, a new face, start from zero, from scratch.

An unknown face.

Love again, blindly.

Brie was a good woman and I did her wrong by breaking up with her so abruptly, but I was hurt, really hurt, dying inside, and I couldn't love again. Not then. Not so soon.

A hot afternoon. I sit in a park, waiting. Waiting for the minutes to go by so that I can get my daughter from school, then wait by the bus stop just so I can take her to her mother's place, then wait at Yu's place for Yu to arrive. Then leave, walk to another bus stop and wait for another bus. Maybe the same bus, same driver; it happens sometimes.

Tomorrow, the same thing, but instead of going home I'll be heading to work.

A life of waiting… for Death to arrive.

24th June 2021

Monotonous days. I spend most of the morning wondering, walking around town. I've got nowhere to go, so much to do. Let's face it; I need my own place, privacy, a place where I can realise my projects, a place where I can meditate.

While I was at Starbucks, 52 Broadgate, I saw Francis again, making his way down the road, head down, lost in his thoughts, in the insanity of the world, maybe the insanity of his own thoughts. I saw him yesterday too, around 7PM, by Pool Meadow Bus Station. I took the bus 14 to town, went to Sainsbury's to get a bottle of Huel for dinner, the vanilla flavour, and when I walked out of the supermarket, I saw Francis a.k.a. NotJesus, making his way up the road. He didn't see me, and even if he did I wonder if he would recognise me. He looked lost as he moved along the city, as if he didn't know where to go or didn't have anywhere to go. Maybe all isn't well in his head.

This morning, while I was walking around town, I felt so sad, so lost, as if I too had nowhere to go. I missed something, I don't even know what. I cried a bit. Maybe I cried for what I'm missing even though I don't even know what I'm missing.

I miss my children, their warmth, their laughter, their cheekiness, their good moods, even their bad moods. I miss what I'm missing every day, what I can never get back. At least yesterday I managed to play for a long time with both my children. It was nice to play with the two of them, to hear their laughter, to laugh along with them. Yu was already at home. She wasn't laughing.

This afternoon, while I was at Yu's place, I got a bit of good news. One of my books got accepted by a small publisher and it might be out before the end of this year. A bit of light ahead. A bit of hope.

It will be nice to see my name in print, one of my books out, and I know that this book won't probably change my life that much (then again, who knows?), but like I've said, it's something, maybe the first step towards a New Life, a new beginning, a New Start, Something Better, and I sure need That. For a long time now, I've been in a dark place, swimming in a lake of tears, and I almost drowned in that lake, a lake filled not only with my tears but also with screens flashing dirty images, images that I saw quite early on in life because there were books filled with those images at my Grandmother's place, images that I told myself I would never show to any of my children because stuff like that is bad and it can corrupt your mind for a long time, maybe even forever if a person isn't careful, but, with the Grace of the Lord, and the love of Christ for us, thanks to a new regained Faith, a Faith that got a bit weaker because of the darkness, I have, finally, *thank you Lord*, managed to get those images out of my head, although, if I'm honest (and why shouldn't I be?) (and I'm not perfect), every once in a while, mostly in times of desperation and loneliness, those images still pay me a visit, but only in my head, and they want me to go online, look at them, get lost in sin, get lost, get lost forever, but I say NO!

Again and again, I say NO!

The world already has enough sin. I must try to be one of the good guys.

Friday, June 25th. A couple of days ago I've noticed that Yu's place is always in a mess. While I was there I grabbed the hoover, cleaned around the place, tidied up in the kitchen, and did Leaf's bed. In the past, when me and Yu were still married, I did everything at home but she always complained that I didn't do enough. Some mornings I would arrive home from work, prepare breakfast for the children, tidy up in the kitchen, sleep for a couple of hours, get up, hoover, prepare lunch and dinner, iron the clothes, and while I was doing all that Yu would be sitting on the sofa all afternoon, playing games on her mobile phone or watching Netflix. And then she would go to bed in the middle of the afternoon because she was tired from doing nothing. I would get ready to go to work and she would still be in bed. Thirteen hours later, I would be home and Yu would still be in bed. What a life. But if I were to get a few hours' rest she would go berserk and call me lazy. Looking back, thank G-d she divorced me.

Jesus said, "You cannot serve G-d and money."

Nowadays we live in a culture obsessed with possessions and Money, a culture that is distancing itself from G-d. I fear the world is reaching breaking point. Sooner or later, hell will be unleashed on us. There's too much sin in the world, and it's getting worse by the day. Men, women, and whatever you call yourself nowadays, are running away from G-d at full speed. But there is hope; there is always hope, because some people that were lost in sin have found their way towards G-d and Christ, and they have left their old sinful ways of life behind. You won't hear about these people on the news. In the eyes of the media these people don't exist, but that's because the media has long ago forgotten G-d and is only obsessed with Money. If you happen to love Christ the Saviour (some of) the world will make fun of you, and turn against you, but didn't they make fun of Christ too? If that happens, you're in good company.

I still have so much to learn. I'm far from perfect. Some of the words I'm writing here shouldn't be written, not by me, not by a follower of Christ. There are a few bad words in here, words that I can never repeat, but I was hurt, really hurt, lied to, and this is just me letting it all out; the pain, the anger, the sadness. After this is written, I won't go back to being the person I used to be.

In the end I will forgive Yu.

I must.

To be forgiven, I must learn to forgive too.

June 27th.

I got up a few minutes after 11AM, took a shower, got changed, and took the 6A bus to the city centre. As always, I took a notebook with me. And a book, too; *The Kybalion* by The Three Initiates. Once in town, I went to Waterstones, browsed through two books; *Blue in Chicago* by Bette Howland and a book about Buddhism and meditation. I didn't buy any of those books but a few hours later I went back to Waterstones to buy the book by Bette Howland. From there I took a short walk to Pool Meadow Bus Station. I go there most Sundays to help out two charities that hand out food to the needy, and I also take a bit of food with me. Julian was there, as was Jeremy. Jeremy took some food with him and then went back to his place to leave the food in the room where he's staying. As for Julian, since he sleeps outside, on the streets, or wherever he can, he just carries his food with him wherever he goes. There was a woman with Julian, a woman I've never seen before. Later I find out that her name is Su.

Su tells me that she's a poet, vegan, and that she's travelling through England, sleeping wherever she can, eating whatever she can (but only vegan stuff), and that she left a bad relationship behind her. She wouldn't tell us where she's from. Only that she wrote poetry, was into Reiki, was vegan, but personal stuff was taboo. I nodded to let her know that I understood. She was wearing a face mask and large sunglasses, but I did see her face, briefly, and it was a pretty face. My friend Peer was there too. Peer is Hare Krishna's and quite a character, but he seems to be a good person. We sat somewhere to talk, me, Julian, Peer and Su. Jeremy joined us too, and later, the three of them, Su, Jeremy and Julian, went to Langar Aid House to get some hot food while Peer went to a nearby park to meditate. As for me, I grabbed my bags and went to another park where I read for a bit. Yu texted me while I was at the park just to find out what holidays I had booked for August so that I could look after the children while she was at work. I had already told her twice what days I had booked off, and I even texted her the dates on WhatsApp, so why was she texting me again?

I couldn't really be bothered to reply but I had to say something so I told her that I didn't know what days I had booked off and that I would have to check on my diary once I was home. And that was that. There was nothing else to say. After our breakup, once we went our separate ways, I still tried to maintain some sort of relationship with Yu, message her every once in a while, but then I saw that it was a mistake, a huge mistake (forget and flee), and that I was trying to resurrect a dead thing. The love was dead and there was nothing I could do about it. The longer Yu was away from my life, the calmer I felt.

I still can't believe she went out with that Colin guy but I'm not surprised that their relationship didn't last that long.

It was a cool afternoon. On the other side of the road, the pub was full with people watching the match between Netherlands and Czech Republic. I still haven't watched a single match of the Euro and I don't think I will. I heard shouts coming from the pub, followed by laughter. I put the book I was reading down and sat there contemplating the world.

After Su, Julian and Jeremy were gone, Peer told me that humanity is going to face a dark age in months to come and that this Invisible Virus is Manmade and a way of controlling the people. He also told me not to get the vaccine and I told him I have no intention of taking it.

As I sat there on my own, absorbing the words that Peer had told me, I was glad to see that there are others out there that think like me and can see the cracks that are appearing in the world.

"The vaccine is poison," Peer said to me just before we went our separate ways. Then he told me that people who get the vaccine won't be able to ascend to the next world and that their souls will be trapped somewhere else, for eternity.

Yu already had the first vaccine. Maybe the second one, too. I never asked her if she had the second one.

Peer told me a few other things, about 5G, the Mark of the Beast on credit cards, mobile phones, computers, etc., but unfortunately I forgot most of what he said, not because it was boring talk but because I was tired.

I sat there in the park, eyes slightly closed, thinking of the state of the world, of what's yet to come, the dark days ahead, and I saw that there's nothing I can do about it, nothing at all apart from waiting. And while we're waiting, the aliens are watching us, probably laughing at us, and I wonder if they're controlling us, too? They're already here, among us, but doing what?

Mind rested, if only for a little bit, I stood up, grabbed my bags, and made my way to work. Briefly, Su came to my mind. I wondered then if I would see her again or if she would be a brief passenger of this journey of mine called Life.

Apocalyptical poet

The journey to find love is a hard journey, a journey that can last for a long time, sometimes a lifetime. The journey to find real love is even harder. But is it worth it?

You tell me.

Isn't love worth everything?

What can we do without love?

How would the world survive without love?

In bed, I close my eyes, hoping that it is all a dream.

I fall asleep while listening to Kelly Howell. Later, I find myself in a strange dream, going up some mountains in Tibet, heading towards a monastery, running from some bad people, looking for a home, a place where I can write some poetry. I find a home in Tibet, on the mountains, inside a monastery. I find a woman there, a Zen woman, a woman that has lived there all her life. In my dream, some bad people are looking for me, but they never find me, and they die, one by one, while I remain in the monastery with my Zen woman, forever, writing poetry, poems about the end of the world, poems about an unstoppable virus, poems about the end of love, poems about chaos and division, and later, in my dream, I am given the chance to leave the mountains, leave the monastery, but I choose not. And then I wake up, to the madness, to a nightmare.

June 27ᵗʰ, 2021

2021 is turning out to be an even worse year than 2020 but I'm not at all surprised by it. Unfortunately, even though I can't predict the future and I'm not a (fake) prophet, I can see that things will get even worse. I wouldn't even be surprised if there was a big war on the horizon, nuclear, apocalyptical, the war to end most wars but not the final war. The final war will be man against man, stick against stone, fighting for a drop of water, a piece of hard bread, mouldy.

Meanwhile, as more people get infected by the Invisible Enemy virus, the ones in power want to vaccinate the entire world, no matter what. But some of us don't want the vaccine. Some of us don't trust those in power. And do the vaccines even work? Only time will tell.

I open my eyes and see my nightmares coming true. Oh dear!

Even though he got both jabs against the Invisible Enemy, journalist Andy Marr still caught the virus last week. *Oh dear!*

We're being told that cases are going up in the UK and that everyone needs the vaccine, and that there will be another lockdown, but it's the same lockdown all over again, the same lie, again and again, and every week the virus seems to mutate, and the media comes up with another name for the virus.

I smell lies. And I see dark days ahead.

I'm watching the madness from a small screen, the madness that is the world today.

My fear is that sooner or later the Invisible Hand will say, "No jab, no job."

And then what?

Then, as always, I'll be in the hands of the Creator.

June 28th, 2021

I grab a new Muji notebook from my desk, a couple of pens, one blue (pen), one black (pen), my shoulder bag, and I leave home. Yesterday Su told me she needed some paper to write on but she didn't have any, so this morning I went through my notebooks and got her a Muji notebook. I have two new Muji notebooks at home and decided to give her one. Now I'm heading to the city centre, hoping to find Su somewhere. She sleeps on the streets, wherever (and whenever) she can, so I might not even be able to find her.

I leave home a few minutes past 11AM and then I spend close to one hour looking for Su but I can't find her. In the end, I end up going to Caffé Nero where I order a latte, and afterwards I sit down and write for a couple of hours on my laptop. It's a grey morning, the sky promises rain, but even if it does rain I don't think it will be that much.

A few minutes past 2PM, I leave the café. I need to pee, and afterwards I need to get my daughter from school. The city centre is quiet. Only a few people out and about. As I make my way towards West Orchards shopping centre, I see Su waiting outside the Central Library. She's waiting for Julian who has gone in to use the bathroom. With her large face mask and big dark sunglasses, she looks like a character out of an apocalyptical sci-fi novel. I go over to say hello to her and to give her the Muji notebook and the pens. I can see my face on her large dark sunglasses. We talk for a bit, but everything about Su, including her real name, is a mystery. I don't want to bother, to be a nuisance, plus soon I will have to get Leaf from school, so I only spend a few minutes with her. If I could, I would have stayed with her for a bit longer, talking about everything and nothing, about the universe and the insignificance of it all, but I really have to go, and she probably has to go somewhere else too even though she's homeless, so we say goodbye, knowing that probably we will see each other again soon.

At the school gates, a Portuguese friend of mine tells me that teachers are getting some special training and being told what parents have been vaccinated and who practices social distancing. She tells me the government is keeping tabs on all of us, dividing us into groups, but for what reason? To better control us, I came to the conclusion. By dividing us into groups and make us fight against each other, the ones in power will have a better chance to control us, because, if we unite, there would be big trouble ahead for the Invisible Hand that control us all.

"Those who haven't been vaccinated, like me and you, will most likely be seen as the enemy," she said.

The yellow star again?

The fear of the past?

Persecution?

Revelation?

Starvation?

Revelation?

The world is changing so dramatically by the day, sometimes by the hour, by the minute, by the second. All that it takes for the changes to happen is for some idiot like former MP Tony to say, "We need to know who has been vaccinated and hasn't." But the words he speaks aren't even his words. He's a puppet, controlled by invisible wires, being told what to say.

The world is changing (and you can't even see the changes because you're too busy reading lies, following liars, worshiping the stars that are controlled by Moloch). People are being split into groups and categories; those who have been vaccinated and those who haven't. Maybe soon there won't be a place in the world for people like me. Already we're being told we can't travel. Ironically, those who have taken the two vaccines can't travel either. Only the Invisible Hand and their puppets and football stars are allowed to travel. The world is a circus and you're a clown. Now go and clap.

But I already knew that days like this would come again and there's nothing I can do about it.

The world is changing, changing at a scary speed, changing into something scary, changing into a place where good morals are seen as weakness, a place where sin is praised, even worshipped.

What's happening now is nothing compared to what's to come.

But what if nothing happens and I'm wrong? If that's the case, even better.

Give me boredom. I'm fine with it. I can live with the boredom. I've got a good imagination. I'm sure I'll be able to handle the boredom.

June 29th, 2021

I met Julian and Jeremy at the Jesus Centre on Lamb Street. I sat down with Julian and had a chat with him while Jeremy played pool with a few other lads. Who would have thought I would be making new friends during –and after- lockdown? These people don't have much; as a matter of fact, a person can even say that some of them have nothing, or close to nothing, but even though they have little they're willing to share the little they have with others, including food. I didn't saw Su in the morning but I saw her in the afternoon, after 7PM, for only a few minutes. Julian told me he doesn't know much about her because she's very private and hardly shares a thing about herself with anyone. She's quite a fascinating character, someone with whom I would like to stay in touch for a long time.

I saw Yu in the morning when I was waiting for her to drop Leaf outside the school gates, and she (Yu) looked to be in a bad mood. Nothing new there and I didn't even bother to say a word to her. I saw her again in the afternoon, for only a few minutes, and, again, I didn't bother to say a word to her. In fact, I didn't even bother to look at her. It's better this way. I don't have anything against her (actually, I do) but I can't just forget what she did to me last year and pretend that nothing has happened. But I don't wish her harm. I do hope that one day she finds some peace of mind and happiness. Something happened to her; her brain "switched", she went a bit crazy, and then, BANG! Goodbye, M÷. She was always a bit crazy but this time she went way over the top, but that's life and I must move on.

30th June, Wednesday

England beat Germany 2-0 last afternoon for the Euro 2020/21. Harry Kane finally scored at the Euro. I'm glad he's finally scoring.

I got up a few minutes after 6AM, had breakfast, took a shower, and then took the 11 bus to Earlsdon. It was a cool morning, not too cold, not too hot, just perfect. So early in the morning, Earlsdon was almost empty. I managed to spend ten minutes with my daughter before she went inside the school. Those ten minutes with her are better than nothing. Too bad I couldn't also see my son but he's going to a different school, further away from where I live.

After I dropped Leaf at school I quickly made my way back to the bus stop. Another 11 bus was arriving at the stop just as I left the school. I quickly run to the bus stop and managed to catch that bus.

I needed to go to town, go to the Portuguese minimarket by 9 Coventry Canal Basin, buy a bottle of Portuguese wine and some sweets because I have been invited to a party at Cassandra's house and I don't want to go empty-handed. A few other friends of Cassandra and Gary will be attending the party. Maybe I'll meet someone, a Zen woman, love.

Love?

Not again.

I got off the bus just outside the Wave, a water park in Coventry, and as I made my way down the road, I saw Su making her way past the Little Tree on Warwick Road. She had a Greggs cup with her, her dark sunglasses on, her large rucksack on her back, and she was still wearing the same old clothes. I wanted to call for her, say hello, maybe buy her breakfast, but I also know that she's escaping something, some sort of pain, and maybe she wants to spend some time alone, so I thought best not to approach her. G-d willing, I will see her again.

Coventry is so small. You meet someone and then you see them almost every day.

I saw Francis yesterday. As a matter of fact, ever since I met him, I've seen him every single. Yesterday, when I saw him, I was on the bus, and there he was, walking along the road, head down, talking to himself.

I sat at Starbucks for a few minutes from where I watched the world go by, life moving at a slow speed, a few people —but not many- rushing past the café, almost running without really going anywhere. 8:42AM and the city was almost empty.

Where was Su going?

What will she do today?

Is she writing?

Last year, while I was going through the separation, and then through the divorce, I had nowhere to go, no place to sit down and drink a coffee, but the world is slowly returning to some sort of normal. But will there be dark days ahead?

Will the left hand of the Invisible Hand bring more chaos to the world?

The Invisible Hand is pushing so many agendas forward, selling more fear, and people like Will Bates are already sponsoring the next agenda, sponsoring fear. The next agenda will be the Climate Change Agenda.

More fear on the way. More restrictions on your freedom. Soon you won't be able to go anywhere. Only the Invisible Hand and their puppets will have that luxury. Later they will tell people that it's okay to keep on changing. It's okay to transform, become some sort of machine. That's when the Transhumanism Agenda will start. And I fear that this new generation will embrace it with open arms.

The Invisible Hand won't rest until they have total control of humanity.

Some people are fighting, protesting, fighting for a good cause, fighting for the right to be human, for the right to believe, but the media never shows those protests on telly. What the world needs is a revolution; a revolution of the mind, the soul, the spirit, a revolution ten times bigger than the French Revolution. The world needs to wake up before it's too late. Maybe it's already too late. Maybe…

While I was still in the city centre, I bumped into Julian outside the Central Library. He was waiting for Su who had gone inside Greggs to refill her cup with hot water. According to Julian, Su drinks a lot of hot water. I sat next to Julian and the two of us waited for Su to return. A few seconds later, I saw her making her way towards us; my apocalyptical poet, dark shades on, face mask on, the mysterious vegan. She said hello and smiled. She has a pretty smile, thin lips, a thin figure.

The three of us stayed there for quite a long time just talking. My phone rang once while I was talking to Julian and Su. I looked at the number. It was Cassio. A few minutes later, it rang again. Cassio again. I let it rang.

A while later, when I was on the 2nd floor of West Orchards Shopping Centre, Cassio called me again. I answered the phone. Big mistake. Cassio needed money. Thirty pounds. He always needs money because he's always broke, and he's always broke because he gambles everything away and buys a lot of junk. I so regretted answering the phone. By now I should have known better. Whenever Cassio calls me repeatedly it's because he needs money, but I can't be lending him money all the time. Ironically he needs to borrow money from me so that he can pay someone else. He still owes me ten pounds. Next time I won't answer the phone. Cassio needs to learn his lesson once and for all.

I read on a site called Anonymous Incision that the majority of people that took the vaccine against the Invisible Enemy will be dead by 2025. Until then, so much more will happen.

Even though I hardly know her, I worry about Su. The streets aren't a safe place for anyone, especially for a pretty lonely woman. I hope that soon she finds some peace of mind and decides to return home. But what if home is the place she's trying to escape?

I got home quite late, a few minutes past 11PM. I'm never home this late but I went to Cassandra's place for dinner and to meet new people. It was a lovely evening, quite enjoyable, a good evening spent with lovely people, and I sure needed it.

We sat outside, wood burning, vegan chilli con carne (Quorn) for dinner, followed by dessert. We spoke for hours, told jokes, laughed loads. Five of us; me, Gary, Cassandra, and two friends of theirs. Maybe, bit by bit, my life is moving forward. I met this woman called Ellie. I really liked her but I know nothing about her. I wanted to ask her something, anything, but I was too shy to start a conversation. I could tell she was a few years older than me but how many? And is she married? Does she have someone?

Thursday, 1ˢᵗ July

A new month, some good news.

A small publisher has agreed to publish my book *Dust*. A contract has been sent to me, and I'll sign it today. It's only a small publisher but at least it's something, better than nothing.

I wrote the book in 2019 and then just left it on the side, almost forgotten. I didn't want to self-publish it on Amazon and sell nothing, or close to nothing. I wanted to wait and see if I could publish it somewhere else. It's only a small book and a small publisher, but I guess I have to start somewhere.

Another morning spent walking aimlessly from place to place, looking at the world and seeing nothing, looking at the world and seeing what others can't see; a future of transhumanists, a sad, cold world.

Bumped into Julian and Su outside Snax in the City, spoke with them for a few minutes, then moved along, towards nowhere. Carlos called me, told me that Grandmother is well, told me he's getting a pay rise, told me he's been married for more than 25 years, told me he misses me, told me he's getting a promotion, etc., etc.

Stopped at Julian Court, facing Regent Street, for a few minutes. I was tired of walking, tired of waiting, but I know that the wait will go on for a bit longer. At the end of it, there will be some rewards. Something to look for.

Carlos told me that a few more people have died from the Invisible Enemy virus, people who have been vaccinated.

"The vaccines are useless," he said.

He's already been vaccinated. My two brothers in Spain have also been vaccinated. Probably, apart from me, everyone in my family has been vaccinated. Actually, my cousin Rogério hasn't been vaccinated, and he doesn't want the vaccine.

The Invisible Enemy is mutating, becoming stronger, and it's not going away, vaccine or no vaccine.

Meanwhile, the Invisible Hand's new agenda is already being put forward at full speed. The Eco Agenda (but I've already mentioned it). More fear to sell. More restrictions on our freedom. Soon we'll be told we can't travel. Again. Already, because of the Invisible Enemy, we can't go anywhere, but football starts can travel everywhere. And the rich cats can travel too. But the "little people" are being told they can't go anywhere. And they clap.

Even poor rich Britney is controlled by the Invisible Hand.

First, you sin.

Then you search for G-d.

You should search for G-d first so as not to sin.

I saw Ellie again, on Earlsdon Avenue North, when I was taking my daughter home. I saw her from across the road and waved at her. She waved back and smiled. She has such a pretty smile. The first time I saw her, which was yesterday, I fell in love with her smile straight away. And today I saw her again. Maybe it's a sign. Or plain coincidence. Once she was out of sight, I thought, "Maybe I should have crossed the road and said something, maybe ask her out for a cup of coffee." I turned around and watched her from afar.

"What if I don't see her again for a long time?" I thought. "Maybe I've wasted my chance."

A person is always thinking, thinking too much, always dreaming, dreaming too much, thinking about love, dreaming about love, but what if love is a lie and we're dreaming in vain, thinking hopelessly about something that might never come our way?

2nd July 2021

Yu texted me last night to let me know that our son Matthew was sick and that he wanted me to go over to her place and look after him so would I mind going over? I could get a few hours' sleep at her place and keep an eye on Matthew, cook him something, etc., and I said, yes, of course.

For the last couple of days Yu has been friendlier towards me, and yesterday she even tried to make small talk while I was at her place, but I didn't have much to say to her so I said as little as possible. What happened between us is now in the past, including the good and the bad, and I do worry about her, how her life is going to be in the future, because, apart from our children, she has no one else, but I'm also moving on with my life, or trying to, and I don't think I would want Yu in my new life. I don't think I could trust her again. She's so unpredictable, sometimes so cold, and a bit mad.

Poor Yu got greedy, decided to get herself a little place in the middle of nowhere, a home that is too small for her and the children (but she couldn't see past the greed), but sooner or later she'll realise that she has made a big mistake. But the mistake was hers, not mine, and I don't want to wait on her or go back to her. Plus there's that "little matter" called love and the truth is I no longer love Yu and I could never fall in love with her again. Love is dead. At least ours is.

Not so long ago, as I went through some journal entries from last year (and even previous years), journal entries that I then used for my novel *The Invisible Hand*, I saw that I went through so much crap because of Yu, endured so much (silent) abuse from her, put up with her coldness and constant mood swings for such a long time, and I certainly wouldn't want to go back to that. Wrong or right, she made her choices, and now the four of us, me, her and our children, have to live with it. Fine. So be it. But I can't go back to "That".

And so, after work, I quickly went to McDonald's for breakfast, went back to my place to get clean underwear and socks, grabbed some food to cook for me and Matthew (and for Leaf and Yu, too), and then took the 6A bus to Yu's place.

When I got there, Matthew opened the door for me. He looked a bit poorly. I kissed my son and told him to go back to bed. I put the food in the kitchen, got changed, checked on Matthew; he was back in bed, and then I grabbed a few hours' sleep.

I was up a few minutes after 11AM, cooked some pasta, tidied up the place, and spent a few hours with my son. I had to quickly go to Earlsdon, get Leaf from school, and then bring her back home.

When I got to school, Leaf was happy to see me. She told me about her day, showed me some new drawings she did, and then she asked, "At home, will you play Roblox with me?"

"Of course," I said.

I felt like a dad then. So happy. A few hours later, I was back at work, a bit tired but so thankful for having spent a few hours with my children.

July 5th

I saw Julian and Su almost every day this week. On Friday I bumped into them in town. On Saturday I saw them in St. Barnabas Church, and yesterday I saw them near Pool Meadow Bus Station, at the flyover, where food is given to homeless people and those in need. Whenever I can, I help out at the flyover. My friend Harry is one of the people in charge, and one day he told me he needed help so now I help out. Su was late arriving so I set some food aside for her and then gave it to Julian so that he could give it to her in case I missed her. When Su finally arrived I gave her more food. She didn't take much. Only fruit, really, so I gave her lots of apples and grapes. Jeremy was there too. He never takes any fruit.

"Too healthy for me," Jeremy always says.

Apart from the bread (there were lots of it), we gave all the food and drinks away.

Even though I hardly know her (as a matter of fact, I don't know her at all), I like Su. I like her as a friend and I would like to remain in touch with her for the rest of my life but that might not be possible. Then again, who knows?

I took some food for me too, just enough for the next two days, and once all the helpers, including me, tidied up, I grabbed my bag, said, "See you later," to Su, Julian, and Jeremy, and from there I made my way towards Coventry Cathedral where I sat down to eat, and later read.

I've mentioned that Su is homeless but she's not really homeless, I think. She's on some sort of journey of self-discovery, going through a change, writing some poetry along the way. It is a journey that can come to an end at any given time; she has no time limit, maybe no one's waiting for her.

I hope life smiles on her. I pray that the Creator always keeps an eye on her, protect her from any wrongdoing. From what I can tell (but I hope I'm wrong), she's already suffered enough.

Near Coventry Cathedral, there was this lady sitting on the bench next to mine. I see her there most Sundays, smoking and browsing through her phone. She looks to be in her late fifties, maybe early sixties, but she still has a good body.

My brother Carlos called me while I was eating. He called to tell me that Grandmother was back at the care home. We had a scare on the previous day because Grandmother wasn't feeling well and had to be taken to hospital. She's 91-years old and we worry about her health. Whatever happened in the past between her and me no longer matters.

The day went by so fast. Before I knew it, it was time to go back to work. I had only slept for two hours. Before 11AM I met Emma by Spon End and got a key for the allotment from her. Bit by it, I'm starting a new life, making new friends, starting again. Life has taught me that is never too late to start again. But there's something missing. Someone missing. Something, someone, but what?

The loneliness is still here, walking alongside me, sometimes dragging me a bit down, but there are days when I need the loneliness so that I can write and dream and think. But eternal loneliness? That might be the end of me.

Because I work alone I managed to get a few hours rest at work.

Tuesday, 6th July

I left work around 6:20AM, then quickly went to McDonald's for breakfast. There were already some people out and about by the city centre. I even saw a couple that I know sitting outside Starbucks on 52 Broadgate, enjoying a cup of coffee. There was only one customer inside McDonald's. I ordered breakfast, waited a few minutes, grabbed my food and drink from the counter, said hello to a worker that I know, and then left.

I ate my breakfast at a nearby park, and a few minutes later, when I was making my way to the bus stop, I saw Su on the other side of the road, opposite the Belgrade Theatre. Right then, we were the only people out on the street. Seconds later, someone jogged past me. I waved at Su and she waved back. She stopped then and waited for me to cross the road. As I made my way towards her, I felt as if we were characters in a sci-fi novel, a novel written by me, a novel where the enemy is a virus that can't be stopped, an Invisible Enemy, Manmade to destroy parts of the world. And sometimes part of me believes that this Invisible Enemy that we're fighting right now was Manmade, created as a bioweapon to bring horror to the world, created to destroy a certain amount of people, created by ruthless people, by someone who's devoid of compassion, maybe an evil government, an evil leader, and only time will tell if I'm right.

Anyway, so early in the morning, and there I was with Su, my apocalyptical poet whom I met at a strange time in the world. We made small talk.

I asked, "Where are you going this early in the morning?"

"I couldn't sleep so I decided to go for a walk," she said. "I was in Solihull yesterday. I wrote a note saying goodbye to everyone and then I left and went to Solihull, but around 6PM everything shuts down and there isn't a single soul on sight."

I was glad she returned to Coventry. In a way, I've got used to seeing her almost every day, but I do hope that soon she returns home.

"Sooner or later, you will have to return home, settle down and start again," I said, adding, "This is no life for anyone, especially for a lady."

Su nodded.

As always, her face and eyes and even her hair were covered. She was wearing a baseball cap, a large face mask, large sunglasses, and the same jeans, jacket, and trainers that she always wear.

"Do you want to grab a cup of coffee or a cup of tea? Or even breakfast? I'll pay for it," I said.

"No. I'm good. But thank you," she said.

While I was speaking with Su I completely forgot about the world, even my problems. Later, once I was on the bus, I thought, "What strange days we're living in. This is like something straight out of a sci-fi novel."

Last year, in January, I started writing a journal, and I even thought, "This is going to be a boring journal," but then came the virus, followed by lockdown, the end of my marriage, moving out, divorce, etc., and I kind of lost my mind, almost lost the will to live, and the world became a prison (for me), a spiritual prison, and my journal became a crazy sci-fi novel. My friend Jemi became on the main characters of the novel, but only right at the end. And talking about Jemi, she too has become a stranger and there's a good chance that I will never see her again.

And while my journal became a sci-fi novel, my life too became a bit chaotic, and my mind started to see danger everywhere, conspiracies everywhere, and I took a step back from the real world and let my imagination take me wherever it wanted to take me. The paranoia became real, and I became the hero of a sci-fi novel, fighting an Invisible Enemy in a loveless world. And Su too became the heroine of her own sci-fi novel, an apocalyptical poet walking along the ruins of a loveless world. We met halfway through the plot and later we would have to go our separate ways but still fight the same enemy. But who was the enemy? Loneliness or the lack of love?

"What about money? Do you need some money? I don't have much with me but I can give you some," I said. I had a five pound note in my wallet, and a few coins too, but that was for laundry, and I didn't mind giving the five pound note to Su.

"No. I'm good. Thank you," she said.

"Are you sure?"

"Yes, but thank you."

One thing I've noticed about Su is that she never asks for anything, never takes more than what she needs, and she looks as if she's always willing to help.

The minutes were flying by, and I still had to go home, get my laundry bag, go to Earlsdon, see Leaf for a few minutes, and then do my laundry.

"I'm sorry, Su, but I really have to go. I still want to see my daughter for a few minutes," I said.

"Okay."

"But I'll see you today at the Jesus Centre," I said.

She nodded and we went our separate ways.

If I could, I would have spent the entire day with Su, have lunch with her, listen to her, to her poetry, and even read some of my crap poems to her, but I really had to go. My laundry was pilling up plus I wanted to see my daughter even if only for ten minutes. And so I left my apocalyptical girl alone, behind. She kind of reminds me of a character from Bolaño's *The Savage Detectives*, a poet walking through a vast desert, gathering pain and experience for her poetry, a lost poet in a world that is losing its soul, a poet that is not so lost because she's finding herself. Even I, during these chaotic, apocalyptical times, am finding myself.

I took a bus home; I can't remember which, 6A, 18, 11, I don't know, grabbed my two bags filled with dirty clothes, put them down again, removed the socks I was wearing, the underwear, got changed again, then left the bedroom, ran to the bus stop, and got to Earlsdon just in time to see my daughter.

Yu was already parked outside the school, stepping out of the car just as the bus I was in was arriving. I was tired but I still had so much to do, and since it was my day off, I wanted to get everything out of the way, and then just enjoy the next two days.

Yu no longer matters (and I know that I'm repeating myself, and if one minute I say I forgive her, the next minute I'll probably badmouth her and say that I hate her). I don't hate her (see what I mean?) (and I do) (see what I mean?), but, as I've said before, if I could I wouldn't have her in my life. That day will come, and once I'm gone, she will miss me.

Laundry done, I headed home, took a shower, got changed, then took the 6A bus to town.

A woman looked me up and down when I entered the bus. She gave me an unfriendly stare because I wasn't wearing a face mask but I had a card saying that I'm exempt from wearing one. Still, she didn't care. If the time ever comes when people will snitch on their neighbours and friends for not wearing face masks, that woman will be a snitch. My colleague Patrick will be one too. At times he reminds me of a Stasi agent; always spying on people, going through peoples drawers at work, etc., but now, because of lockdown and due to the fact that the building where we work is almost empty, he no longer does that, but there was a time when he was always snooping around, constantly spying on people, even on his neighbours. He always thinks he's mightier than might, squeaky clean, but he never sees his wrongdoings.

I sat on the seat opposite that woman. She looked away and went back to her phone. Looking around me, I saw that almost every single passenger was glued to their phones. The machine is constantly with us, always active, always demanding our attention, and there will come a time when humanity will "transform", emerge with the machine, become a part of the machine, give their lives and souls to the machine. That will be the time when humanity will slowly die. No species last forever, not even humans. Not even the machine. Sooner or later, everything comes to an end. Everything dies.

I got off the bus by Belgrade Theatre. Only a few hours ago I'd been on the other side of the road chatting with Su. I looked at my watch. A few minutes past 12PM. People everywhere, crossing the road, carrying bags of shopping, going to coffee shops, home, wherever. People running with no place to go. A couple of young Asian women walked past me. Both of them, so young, so thin, so beautiful. And too young for me. I was getting old. A few more months and I would be fifty. Then what? Yu took will be fifty soon, in four months' time.

I made my way up the road, saw Francis on the other side of the road, making his way down the road, head down, maybe down on his luck, down, down, down. I see Francis almost every single day but I don't think he remembers me. The other day he asked me if I had a lighter and I told him I don't smoke. He showed no signs of recognising me even though, only a few days ago, he was hugging me and telling me to take care.

A bus stopped outside the Salvation Army building. So many people stepped out, only two went in. I took a right, walked past a man sleeping on the grass, two empty cans of beer by his side. Another thin young Asian woman walked past me. She looked like a model. She was wearing black Adidas trousers, white trainers, a white T-shirt, and a long black coat. It was too hot for that coat.

I crossed the road, sat down, and waited for the Jesus Centre to open. I wanted to write. I wanted to read. I wanted to be somewhere else, but where?

I sat there looking at the windows facing me, the wall, the people walking past. A few minutes later, Jeremy arrived. It was good to see a familiar face. He sat next to me, rolled a cigarette, a Polish lad came over to where we were, asked Jeremy for some tobacco, said hello to me, rolled his cigarette, thanked Jeremy for it, and then sat somewhere else. Two other blokes arrived. We were all waiting for the centre to open, waiting to connect with other people, waiting on better days.

"We're all the same," I thought as I sat there with Jeremy. "Regardless of race, colour, gender, religion, if we look deep inside, we'll see that we're all the same. It's just that some of us get lost, some get greedy, some get corrupted by evil. On second thought, maybe we're not all the same."

I looked at the watch.

"Let's go inside," I said to Jeremy.

We got up and went inside the Jesus Centre.

I ate a sandwich and a bag of crisps, and drank a cup of coffee. Jeremy ate a sandwich, drank a cup of tea, and waited for someone to arrive, someone with whom he could play pool with. A few more men came in, men of all places, of all races; Peru, Poland, Nigeria, Pakistan, England, Romania; we were all in there to forget, remember, start again, or simply rest from the outside world. Julian and Su arrived shortly afterwards. Su was the only woman in the room. I waved at her and she came over to where I was. Julian grabbed something to eat and a cup of coffee before joining us.

On that afternoon, for the next hour or so, I got to know Su a bit more. She told me she left a bad relationship behind. Children too. She's a mother but she's not in touch with her children.

She read me a couple of her poems. Poems about changing, new beginnings. Poems about a poet that is searching, a poet that is her, Su, the savage detective, the missing character of Bolaño's masterpiece, an apocalyptical poetess travelling through a country that has been affected by an Invisible Enemy. A fearless poet, surviving on water, fruit and vegetables.

I read her a poem by Hai Zi, that long gone Chinese poet, a lost poet born in a small village in the Anhui Province, China. Hai Zi, gone but not forgotten.

I told Su about my divorce, how I spent months crying and even thought about suicide.

She said, "No. Don't think about it."

She told me how she's finding herself, going back to the person she used to be many years ago, before…

Before heartbreak.

Before giving herself body and soul to a selfish person.

Before…

I nodded.

A lot of us were changing, going back to who we used to be before…

Before heartbreak.

Before giving ourselves to selfish people.

We all ended up in Coventry, locked in an Invisible Prison.

That reminded me of a book by Ben Okri called *The Freedom Artist*.

We were all searching for a way out. And a way back in. A way back into the spiritual world, back to being One with G-d.

G-d is Love.

The enemy (of G-d) (of Love) is Greed.

There are times when it looks as if Greed is winning the battle but G-d always has the winning hand. We just have to trust Him.

"Those days are gone, I hope. Now I want to live, become some sort of monk, write a bit more, become the person I always wanted to be," I said.

"You can," Su said.

"I'm trying," I said

I liked listening to her, being there with her. She's like no woman I've ever seen. Then again, no two people are the same.

But it was almost time to go. I had to get my daughter from school, take her back to her mother's place, wait for Yu to arrive home from work, then go back to my bedroom, finish typing the novel I was working on, eat, sleep, wait, before…

Before Love comes looking for me.

Before the beginning of a New Life.

I didn't want to leave Su but I really had to go.

"I'll see you again, soon, I hope," I said.

"You probably will," she said.

And so I left. I left her there, sitting alone, my apocalyptical poet feasting on fruit, my apocalyptical poet at the end of the world.

But maybe the world won't end.

And maybe later we'll go back to some sort of normal. For now, because of greed, the media keeps on selling fear, not caring about the mental health of some people. The Invisible Hand controls the media, and they want you to fear everything, including your family and friends. And you buy what they're selling.

People like me, Jeremy, Su and Julian couldn't care less about what the media has to sell.

Why the greed?

Why so much greed?

How much is enough?

How much money is enough?

I took the 11 bus back to Earlsdon, one of Su's poems still echoing on my mid. A poem about change, new beginnings.

The world is changing. Will there be a new beginning?

The next agenda is already being planned.

The Eco-Agenda is the next agenda.

More fear.

More fear to sell.

And the people will buy it.

It's becoming repetitive, not to mention boring (and I'm repeating myself; nothing new there), but some people buy everything that is being sold to them by the media.

Wednesday, 7th July 2021

Early in the morning, I get a call from Yu. Leaf is feeling a bit poorly so she won't be able to go to school. I'm already in Earlsdon when Yu calls me.

"I need to go home, get my laptop bag and a few other bits, and then I'll go to your place," I say.

"Okay," Yu says.

In the end, Yu also stays home, working from home, but I still go over to her place, cook lunch and dinner for her and our children ("What am I doing here?" I think while I run around Yu's place), tidy up around the place, but Yu doesn't even thanks me for lunch and dinner. I cook my food, not hers. I bought some food from Sainsbury's and took it with me.

Yu wants to take and take and take, but never to give. The world doesn't work like that. You receive but you also have to give, or else Life will take it from you.

Yesterday, after I left Yu's place, I saw one of her religious friends arriving at her place with some tools. Yu wants people around her, working for her, giving, giving, giving, but she never wants to give.

One day... BOOM!!... loneliness.

But I hope not.

I hope Yu's not lonely.

I hope she finds someone, a good man whom she can be happy with.

I don't really hate her (and I do –but I don't). I'm just angry. Right now (and maybe this anger will last for a bit longer), as one would expect, I'm a bit angry with her, but I used to love her and I wouldn't want to see her sad.

I take the 6A bus home, drop my laptop bag at home, say a quick hi to Liz the landlady, a good friend of mine whom I met at the shul in Birmingham, and then I take the 6 bus to the city centre. I want to sit somewhere, alone, and write. I want to be alone with my thoughts and memories, with my pain and angst, alone like some poet of doom, some poet who has lost the will to live, Romeo without his Juliet, Dante in search of Beatrice, Verlaine desperate for absinthe.

A few minutes past 6PM and the bus is almost empty.

"Where's everyone?" I wonder.

Probably home, getting ready for the match between England and Denmark. I hope England wins and reach the final, and then beat Italy on the final, but, as always, the Italians have a really strong team and I can't see anyone beating them. If England gets to face Italy on the final I think we'll need speed up front, maybe start Grealish and Rashford, and give people like Kane a break. I don't think Kane has been that great and he looks as if he needs rest. Too bad Jamie Vardy isn't in the team. I really like him as a player.

I travel all the way to Pool Meadow Bus Station where I quickly renew my travel card. As of yet, I still don't have a car. I might not buy one this year.

"Better days are coming. I can feel it," I think while I'm still at the station.

I've sent a few stories to some magazines. Let's hope at least one of them gets accepted. And soon, hopefully in the next few months, my book *dUST* will be published.

I leave Pool Meadow Bus Station and make my way up the road, past Sainsbury's, past a few shops, past a pub that is still almost empty, and when I reach the Lady Godiva statue facing Starbucks in Broadgate, I see Julian on the distant horizon, sitting on the benches outside Snax in the City. Maybe Su and Jeremy are there with him too but I don't go over to say hello to them. In fact, I think I see Su, briefly.

I came to the city centre so that I can get some writing done and I must get my priorities right. Part of me wants to go over and say hello to my friends, see other people, but then I wouldn't get anything done.

I move along, down the road, past empty benches and closed shops, and I sit on a bench near Argos.

I stay there for close to one hour, just writing and thinking.

When the city starts to get noisier and crowded with football fans, I make my way out of there and catch a bus home. Once home, I meditate for a bit before going to bed.

I sleep on the floor, on a sleeping bag on top of a yoga mat. I've been sleeping like that for quite a long time; it's good for my back, but I don't always sleep on the floor.

Thursday, 8th July

Early rise, breakfast, shower, and then I quickly head to Earlsdon just so I can see my daughter for 5-10 minutes before she goes to school. Then I head to Snax in the City. I fancy a cup of coffee and more time alone so that I can write. I could always write at home but I don't really feel at ease in the house where I'm living and that's why I don't spend a lot of time in there. It's not a bad home to live in, but it's not a place I like to call home either. I only ended up there because of my divorce but later I would like to get my own place, a small apartment where my children can come and stay with me every once in a while.

I catch the 1 bus outside Earlsdon Library. Only two people inside the bus, both female, both younger than me. One of them is reading something by Deepak Chopra. The other is browsing through her mobile phone. The road is busy with traffic, a contrast to a few months ago when there was hardly any traffic on the road. I think of the future, of my life a few months from now; what will I be doing? Where will I be living? Will I be loving someone?

But I'm thinking too much about the world, about materials, about needs, which is only normal, one might say, but I need to remain with G-d, stay with Christ, embrace my faith, embrace faith.

For the last few months I've been embracing a different way of life. Maybe embracing is the wrong word. I've been searching for it, a new life, a quiet life, a quieter life, a life where I'm a cross between a monk and a writer. I'm almost there, or so I think, or I would like to believe that I'm almost there (but I still feel a bit lost, a bit lonely), but there are a few things still missing. But what?

What's missing?

I decide to go to Snax in the City for a cup of coffee. The lady behind the counter is Romanian. I surprise her with the little Romanian that I know.

They serve big breakfasts at Snax in the City, and their coffee isn't bad either.

I've cut down on the caffeine. Some days I don't even touch the stuff, but this morning I fancy a cup of coffee.

I take a seat close to the entrance, and then I catch up on some writing.

A few minutes pass by and I see Su walk past the café, carrying her large rucksack, wearing the same clothes, the same hat, the large sunglasses, the face mask that is too large for her thin pretty face. She doesn't see me and I wonder where she's going.

A few workers have arrived and they're getting ready to open their food vans. There's a variety of food vans in that area selling different foods; Japanese food, Chinese food, vegan, pork batches, big German sausages, jacket potatoes, etc., and they all seem to do good business. I like the Japanese van, named Tokyo Express, on 2 Market Way. I've been there a few times and had their fish balls with curry. Coventry has (almost) everything that I need. I just need to find that special someone. I thought Yu was that someone. I still remember the first day I met her. She looked so pretty, so innocent, so fragile. Ten seconds with her, I thought, "I'm going to spend the rest of my life with this woman."

I guess I was wrong.

We went to a Burger King for lunch. Afterwards we took a long walk around London. I carried her laptop bag for her. It was a heavy bag. A few hours together and it looked as if we had known each other all our lives. By the end of the afternoon we were a couple and I decided straight away not to look at other women. Like I've said before, I thought Yu was the one; my eternal partner, but I was wrong. And even though I hate her, I really don't hate her. What happened between us had to happen, and it happened for a reason, a reason that none of us knows why (maybe the gods of Life were bored and decided to give our lives a new chapter), and I must move on and forgive, because, if I want to move on, really move on, I need to forgive, and if I want to be forgiven for past sins, I need to learn how to forgive.

I thought Yu would be my eternal muse, and she did became the inspiration for two characters in a collection of novels that I wrote, and maybe later I might write about her, again and again, but to be honest, I just want to forget her, erase her out of my life, not completely because we have children together, but I do want to see less of her, have minimal contact with her, not because I hate her, which I don't; I used to, for only a short time (I'll contradict myself later on), but I moved on. Okay, enough of Yu. I'll return to her later on.

I wrote for a few minutes.

A thin, black man, dressed entirely in white, looking high on something, entered the café and begged, really begged, to use the bathroom. He went downstairs, where the toilet is, and seconds later he was back upstairs, saying that he couldn't use the bathroom, and left the café. He started to dance outside, pacing the entire area as if he was possessed, or high on something, and just as I was watching him, Su arrived.

"From Yu to Su," I thought.

She left her rucksack on a bench and came inside the café. And then she saw me.

She sat facing me. Her rucksack was still outside, on a bench, as was the thin black dude. He was dancing, then walking around, back to dancing.

"You better bring your bag inside, just in case," I said.

At first Su was a bit reluctant to do it, saying that the rucksack was okay, but then she went outside to get the rucksack, and afterwards sat with me for close to one hour. I offered to buy her breakfast but she said she was okay. In the end I got her a cup of hot water and another cup of coffee for me.

The café worker knew Su and her tastes, and she knew straight away who the hot water was for.

I told Su about *The Savage Detectives*, what the book was about, and I promised to get her a copy of that book. I asked her if there was anything she needed and she told me she needed a carrier bag because the one she had was getting worn out. We spoke about the travels of Bolaño and Mario Santiago Papasquiaro, and I told her how Bolaño went from being a poet to a writer because he could make a better living as a novelist. She told me she had two books with her; *Thirteen Reasons Why* by Jay Asher and *Angel* by L. A. Weatherly. We spoke about literature, travelling, the vaccine, the Invisible Enemy, the Invisible Hand, the New Agenda that will come after the Invisible Enemy, how the media sells fear just so it can make a profit and keep people caged in an open prison.

Like me and Julian, Su refuses to take the vaccine. No one knows what's really in the vaccine and I don't like how they keep putting pressure on the people to get vaccinated.

Last night members of the Royal Family were watching the match between England and Denmark and there was no talk about the Invisible Enemy, social distancing, face masks, and I bet that the prince who came all the way from California or wherever the hell he's living didn't have to quarantine. So, it's one rule for them, one rule for us, just as always it has been.

Su agreed with everything I was saying. She could see the lies between the lines, sold to us by the Invisible Hand.

Julian arrived later on. I bought him a cup of coffee from one of the food vans and we chatted for a bit. We spoke about the crimes of the Invisible Hand, monster Epstein, and how so many rich cats were involved with monster Epstein and will probably get away with (literally) murder. It's a mad world we're living in, a lot worse than Sodom and Gomorrah, I tell you. But the media won't tell you this. They won't tell you how they're corrupting the souls of the innocent. Instead they sell you fear and lies while being paid by the Invisible Hand.

Friday, 9th July

A few minutes after 6:30AM. I'm making my way towards the bus stop when I see Su walk past the Litten Tree. I call for her. I have the carrier bag for her and a copy of *The Savage Detectives*.

"It's amazing how we seem to bump into each other randomly," I say.

"It's meant to happen," she says.

We speak for only a few minutes but I'm tired and I need to go home and get some sleep.

Su tells me she slept in a nearby park, on a bench, and that Julian is sleeping on a bench near Argos. And that's it.

Su goes somewhere for a walk, maybe to write, while I head home.

Love dies, and afterwards one lover takes everything and quickly moves on while the other collects the pieces of a broken heart and moves nowhere even though he/she is constantly on the move. It's the illusion of the movement; you're going everywhere and, at the same time, you're going nowhere.

To reach your destination, first you have to mend your broken heart.

Some people die along the way, never to complete the journey. It's a journey that takes you through the Dark Night of the Soul, a journey of immense pain where you feel (spiritually) disconnected from everyone and everything, a journey where you feel completely lost even if you're always on the move, a journey where you can either die or be reborn, a journey where you must close your eyes and travel in the dark.

When I went through my "dark journey", I felt as if Life and G-d had betrayed me, and as if I had been thrown into a dark abyss, an abyss of godless emptiness, and I stayed in the dark for a long time; I stayed in the dark for months, constantly crying, constantly on the move and going nowhere (the illusion of movement while going through the Dark Night of the Soul), asking the Darkness and the Divine, "Why am I here? Why did You give me life and then abandon me? What is the point of it all? Why the suffering? Why? Tell me, WHY?"

I got no answers. Or maybe I wasn't listening.

Love dies, or goes into hibernation for a long time, and while one partner quickly moves on and takes everything, the other feels lost and empty, and then becomes a poet or a writer. Or a ghost.

Like Su, I became a ghost. Or a ghost-like figure, constantly on the move while going nowhere. And I almost quit everything and went to live on the streets. I actually thought about it.

I gave away a lot of my belongings, bought a sleeping bag, and even asked Cassio if I could leave some stuff at his place. When he said yes, I almost quit the rest and went to live on the streets. In the end I found a bedroom to rent at a friend's house but I would like to move out soon.

I'm getting old and I need my own place, somewhere where my children can come and stay with me more often, a place where I can just be.

Love dies, or takes an indefinite break, and while one of the lovers laughs, the other cries.

Love died and you went on a long journey, down a dark path, a path where the ghosts of sad lovers kept you company, a path where the ghosts of deceased lovers told you to quit: life wasn't worth the pain, love was a disillusion, or, even worse, an illusion, some people even called it a lie, the biggest lie of all, a lie that started in the Garden of Eden with Adam and Eve, a lie that wasn't love but lust, two different matters all together, and now you were crying, because of love, dying, because of a lie, and the Divine Being that you called Father, King, Holy Lord, had shut his Eyes and blocked His ears, so no one was really listening to you, and no one was watching over you.

You were lost; moving but going nowhere: the illusion of movement, the disillusion of hope; you were going everywhere, walking with tears in your eyes, walking on tired legs, and while you were going nowhere, and crying everywhere, your punisher was at home, eating the food you bought, playing games on her stupid smartphone, watching Netflix, chatting with her religious friends online, probably badmouthing you, playing the victim, lying not to herself neither to her friends but to the Creator, and she was planning a new life, designing it, buying it (in part, with your money), and while you were lost in the Dark Night of the Soul, she was running towards the Deception of the Lie, running and laughing, running but going nowhere: Ah, the illusion of movement; going nowhere because she was going against Life, Love, Nature, and the Divine, while you, who was lost, without even knowing it, you were being led towards a New Life, a Life that would start with Hope, followed by Dreams, until, finally, you would reach Love.

Love...

Love doesn't die.

It can't die.

153

Love is everything.
Jesus is Love.

John 3:16

I came to Jesus last year, while I was still going through my own Dark Night of the Soul. I fell into His path by accident, or maybe it was meant to happen. Or maybe He guided me towards Love, Faith, and Hope just so He could say, "Stop! Stop right now, have a rest, and leave your cross behind. I carried the cross so you wouldn't have to. So now, rest. Rest in Me."

Saturday, 10th July 2021

Emma, my partner at the allotment, has released her first song with her group. I'm really happy for her. She plays the drums, does a few of the vocals, and also writes a few songs.

Sunday, 11th July

I went to Holy Trinity Church for the morning service. A good service, met some new people, saw a priest that I had met before. First time I met him was at Coventry Cathedral and he's always been kind to me, always invited me to go back to church, join some people on Zoom so that I wasn't alone, and when he saw me at Holy Trinity Church he came over to say hello. That was nice of him.

My friend Peter, who sings in the choir, also came over to say hello and see how I was. I need to find new people, church-going people, make new friends, settle down.

Saw Julian, Su and Jeremy in the afternoon. Only spoke with Su for a few minutes. Later, Julian told me that Su might be leaving Coventry soon, maybe travel down to London and who knows where else. I hope she's happy (and safe) wherever she goes.

Julian told me that he's also thinking about leaving Coventry, maybe travel south. Afterwards me and Jeremy went for a short walk around the city centre, spoke about some people that we know who are always arguing with others and getting into fights. We went our separate ways by Pool Meadow Bus Station. I headed towards the benches by the Cathedral while Jeremy made his way to Snax in the City where some of his friends hang out.

Two days without seeing my children. I miss them both so much.

Finished reading Mallo's *Nocilla Lab*.

For the last three days my brother Carlos has been giving me short calls, one ring and the phone goes off. He wants me to call him so I called him this afternoon. He told me he's self-isolating for 14 days because one of his colleagues has the Invisible Enemy virus symptoms or whatever.

"But I'm okay. I've done the test, it came out negative, I've taken the two vaccines, and I still have to stay at home for 14 days," said Carlos.

From what he told me, people get fined if they go out during confinement and that some people grass out on others. It's the PIDE all over again.

"Some people in Portugal tend to forget the years of Salazar and the PIDE. It's amazing how people are so easily brainwashed by the media and the lies sold by the media," I said. "No lessons are learned from the past."

Carlos agreed with me.

In places like Lisbon a person isn't allowed in unless you had the two vaccines and a negative test certificate.

A prison is being built around us, the biggest prison of all, and our freedom is being taken away from us, but the majority of people seem oblivious to it. They don't want to fight for their freedom, but sooner or later we will have to take a stand for our freedom and scream, "LIBERTADE!"

The fight is real, the enemy is powerful, but we can't cross our legs and arms and hope that someone else will fight for us. Freedom doesn't work that way. Freedom is earned, not expected.

A friend of mine sends me news from South America, tells me what's happening in Cuba, and I know that the revolution will also reach England. Actually, it's already here, but the mainstream media isn't talking about it.

Tuesday, 13ᵗʰ July

Su is leaving tomorrow morning.

I met her at the Jesus centre on Lamb Street at around 13:05PM and she told me she's moving on. First, if all goes according to plan, she's going to travel through the canal and head to Rugby. Afterwards she's going to make her way to London. Who knows where she'll go after that?

I spoke with her for close to one hour. Julian and Jeremy were there too, at the Jesus Centre. Sooner or later Julian will leave Coventry too. Me and Jeremy have no plans of leaving Coventry but life can change so suddenly, and, before you know it, new plans are made, a new life starts, and a person moves on. But for now, I don't think I'm going anywhere.

I will miss Su. She's an odd person; not eccentric, just odd. Or maybe she's not even that odd. I hope that one day we'll get in touch again.

We hugged just before I left the Jesus Centre. Two big hugs. Tomorrow she starts a new journey. The same old journey but a new path. May G-d be with her through her travels.

I made a new friend at the Jesus Centre. His name's Paulo and he's from Peru. He's been living in Coventry for decades. Facially, and even the way he talks, he reminds me of an old friend from Brazil.

Had a cup of coffee today.

No coffee tomorrow…maybe.

Wednesday, July 14th. I go online to check the news and see that the media is selling more fear. And the people are buying it. It never ends. Now the media is saying that the people will need vaccine passports to go shopping, to go to bars, events, coffee houses, etc. This is a form of putting more fear on people and to force us all to get vaccinated, but not everyone, including me, wants the vaccine. But the media doesn't care. It never cared. It says it does but it doesn't. It's all a lie. It only cares about greed.

France (and its idiotic leader) is already making vaccines mandatory for health workers, and hundreds of thousands of people are rushing to set up appointments to get vaccinated after the (idiotic) French president warned that the unvaccinated would face restrictions.

Before you know it, they might even demand that the unvaccinated wear some sort of star or label on their chest so that they can get distinguished from the vaccinated. The media loves this. It allows it to sell even more fear. How disgusting.

I came to Birmingham for a day out. For now, while I can, let me go out for a bit. Hopefully the unvaccinated won't have any stupid restrictions in England but a person never knows what's around the corner.

I took the train from Canley to Birmingham New Street. When I got out of the train, I saw that the station was full, and only me and another lad weren't wearing face masks. But no one seemed to care, and no one gave me any dirty looks. People were too busy with their lives, lost in their own thoughts, or just enjoying a day out. I was actually supposed to go to Redditch to see a friend, but the meeting got cancelled, and since I'd already bought the ticket I decided to come to Birmingham.

My first stop was Wayland's Yard on 42 Bull Street where I ordered a flat white. I like their coffee and I haven't been there for more than 15 months.

I will visit a few shops and get some sushi before heading home.

For now I'll try not to let this Invisible Enemy and the Greedy Media to influence my way of living. I've already been through so much crap in the last few months and now I want some sort of rest, a bit of peace. Maybe I shouldn't write this book because it will upset some people, but aren't we living in a free society? Shouldn't a person be allowed to write what he or she wants/feels? Should freedom of expression be banned and only be given to those who follow a certain way of thinking?

Left or Right, aren't we all human beings?

Let's not let the media split us into categories. After all, we're all the same. We're all children of G-d, children of Light, human beings in search of a perfect life, a happy ending.

Su comes to mind while I'm drinking my coffee. By now, she's probably making her way towards Rugby.

Going through the news, I see that some French health workers are furious about having to be forced to have the vaccine and are thinking about quitting their jobs. They say that it's against their human rights having to be forced to be vaccinated, and they are right. Of course, (some of) the snowflake generation will go against these workers, but this new generation is being brainwashed by a disease called social media. As for me, I'll say no to the vaccine even if, later on, it might mean that I will lose a lot.

For now I'll wait.

I'll wait on better days.

I'll wait on the Star People; maybe they will come soon, to save some of us, those who are deemed worthy to be saved.

You can't forgive.

You can't forget.

Not yet.

You can't forgive her for what she has done, for leaving you with nothing.

You spend the morning in another city, going from shop to shop, looking at books, eating sushi, but the hurt and betrayal is still on your mind, and you know that it will be a long time before you can forgive the one who hurt you.

You saw her yesterday, only briefly, and you couldn't even look at her.

That face you once loved is now so ugly that you can no longer bear to look at her.

You're looking for something, for a new life, a New Life, and Yu can no longer be part of that New Life even if the two of you have two children together. She's your Kryptonite, poison to your eyes. Eventually, with time, you will forgive her (and maybe you already have), but you also want a bit of distance from her.

She's ceasing to exist.

She's becoming a chapter that you must close. Put an end to it.

She'll move on (she already has, and she's building a home for herself, in part with some of your money, but that's okay), and you're moving on as well. But, for now, she's there, if only briefly, in your life.

She's the snake in your garden. Shake it off. Eat another apple. Find yourself another woman. Or wait. Wait for a bit. Enjoy life.

Be Life.

Be Alive.

Here we go again...

Is the apocalypse closer than we think?

Yesterday I read that NASA predicts a "wobble" in the moon's orbit may lead to record flooding on Earth. Worldwide flooding. Chaos. Death. Apocalypse.

No wonder some billionaires want to escape to a new planet. Again, as it has happened so often in the past, maybe nothing will happen. Maybe they're only selling fear. And if something does happen there's nothing I can do about it apart from waiting.

And so I wait... for the Star People to come to my rescue.

19:00PM. I'm still waiting... for nothing.

I'm sick of waiting.

The darkness visits me while I'm waiting.

I feel as if I'm living for nothing, as if I have nothing to give to the world, as if I have nothing to live for.

I'm a lonely man staring at the emptiness of his soul, at an emptiness that is probably not even there; it doesn't exist, but at this moment I feel so empty, as if there's nothing to live for.

I've been out since 7:30AM, going places, moving around and going nowhere. I've got nowhere to go, no one to see, no one to be with.

I'm living on empty, living an empty life.

I feel as if I'm dying, a slow death. There's no bleeding and yet I hurt so badly.

This pain is eating me inside.

I feel like a walking dead man.

Almost a ghost.

Invisible.

Invisible.

Invisible.

I don't exist.

Don't look at me.

Don't look.

Don't.

I sat outside All Souls Church in Kingsland Avenue, drank a bottle of Huel, vanilla flavour, and watched the people walk past me, and as I looked, I searched for a friendly face, for someone that I know. Meanwhile Yu was at home, resting, enjoying herself, waiting for more, waiting on more, waiting for more people to give her more. And while she was waiting for more, I was hoping for a bit, praying for it, for a tiny bit, something, a little bit of hope

After a while, I got up and caught the 11 bus home. I needed to write, get my life in order, move on, stop crying.

How long does it take for someone to get over a divorce, lies, betrayal, pain?

At home, a bit of good news. The signed contract for my book has arrived. Life is moving on, at a slow speed, but at least it's moving on.

Tomorrow morning, I'll get up early and go straight to the allotment. I need a bit of "me time".

Thursday, 15th July

Came to McDonald's on Alvis Retail Park for a quick cup of coffee before heading to the allotment. The allotment is only a couple of minutes away from McDonald's. The service was terrible. This short, overweight girl turned to me and shouted, "Where's your mask?"

She was one of the workers. Ugly, probably bitter because of the way she looks.

When she saw my "exempt from wearing a mask" badge, she looked away and sheepishly retreated. The Invisible Enemy is affecting a lot of people's brains by making them stupid.

It took forever for my drink to arrive, and when it did (arrive), it was served by the same ugly, bitter girl that shouted at me.

"Here's your drink," she said, almost angrily. She really needs to learn some manners.

"Can I have two sugars and some milk, please?" I asked.

Good thing my manners haven't been affected by the virus and the fear.

July 16th

End of lockdown next week, or so they're telling us, but I think it's all a lie. They will give us a bit of freedom, then tell us that there are more people getting infected and that we need to stay home. Again.

My fear (and suspicions) is that they will come for the children before autumn, just before the school year is about to start, and demand that every child be vaccinated. Already someone spoke about that on YouTube, saying that the ones in power are coming for the children. Scary days await us all.

Yesterday it looked as if Yu wanted to speak with me but I've got nothing to say to her. She said something that I really didn't catch, and she used a soft, humble tone, and later, when I was already outside, she said something else, and, again, she used a soft speech, but I ignored her and kept on walking. She still can't see the damage she has done to me and our family, and the pain she caused me. And why the soft speech now? Is she lonely?

I can't just forget how, last year, when we were still living together, she kept texting me at work, telling me to move out, sending me links for bedrooms and studios that I could rent, and while I was paying for our rent and our food, she was paying for her new home, buying new furniture, planning a new life without me, killing me slowly, and now she's trying to be all nice? To hell with you, Yu. You're a snake. A venomous, poisonous viper.

The more I write about last year, the more I hate Yu.

When I'm at her place, I can't even look at her face.

I look at her sideways, always avoiding her face, and I try to spend as little time possible as I can with her. Once (if) I get what I want, I will cut Yu out of my life.

Listening to Van Halen's *You're No Good* while writing this down. The song is just perfect for what I'm writing. Next track, Gary Numan's *Change Your Mind*.

Tired from a 12-hour shift, the tired father waits outside the school's gates just so he can see his daughter for five minutes. I'm that tired father. For now, I'll take what I can. Later, I'll be given more. But I forgive Yu. I'm not perfect myself. I'm still learning, making mistakes along the way, learning and praying; asking for forgiveness.

To be forgiven, I must learn to forgive.

I no longer miss Yu's plump body or sweet vagina. I couldn't see myself making love (sex) to her again, not even if the flesh was desperate for it. She was a lousy lover; lazy and cold. I would go down on her, again and again, but she would hardly ever do a thing for me. Even when it comes to sex, she wants to take, never to give.

Repent, repeat, repent, repeat, repent… Stop repeating and repenting. And then start living.

It looks as if the Invisible Enemy vaccine isn't doing its job well as a number of people are currently seriously ill with the Invisible Enemy virus in South Wales despite having received both doses of the vaccine. And Israel is already talking about rolling a third vaccine because there is extreme concern that the people who received the vaccine earlier on are now getting infected with the new mutation of the Invisible Enemy.

Dream #1

I dreamt I was at Yu's place, and she was there with our children, shouting at me, demanding that I leave. Her face was a mixture of bitterness and hatred. The dream was a warning, a way of telling me that Yu won't change for a long time and that I must put aside any crazy ideas of ever getting back together with her.

In the dream, when she was shouting at me, I simply shrugged my shoulders and walked away. It was the smartest thing to do. Maybe that's what the dream was telling me to do; just walk away.

Dream #2

I dreamt about my sister Linda whom I haven't seen in more than a decade. My sister lives in Australia and I've only seen her once.

In my dream, the two of us were living in Australia, working side by side, sitting at the same desk, facing one another, typing away. Outside, the sun was shining, and children were playing in the back garden. A lot of children. There were two other women in the house. One of them was cooking while the other was making coffee.

That was it.

A boring dream, just the kind of dream I like to have.

Protests in France. A demon in power, forcing the vaccine on the people.

Protests in Cuba. Demons in power, killing the people.

Tomorrow, protests in London.

The media keeps quiet about it. And while you clap, billionaires are going to space, spoiled footballers are going to private islands, politicians are having affairs, and you're being told to stay at home, don't touch, don't hug, shut the hell up, and clap. Yes, don't forget to clap.

A mad, crazy, insane world, getting worse by the day. They're coming for the children next. We need a Saviour. Who can save us from this madness?

Trump is making some sort of a comeback, but he isn't the saviour. And neither is Zombie Joe.

Poor Joe is a puppet. He looks as if he has absolutely no control over anything as if he is about to fall asleep. Some days I can't even understand a word of what he's saying.

Mad people in power. An Invisible Hand pulling the strings. Clowns in power. Clowns clapping. A bloody circus where the righteous aren't allowed to say a word.

Matthew 10:23

July 17th, 2021

I came to visit Cassio and I already regret it. As always, his life is a mess.

He still owes me £40.00, and he owes a lot of money to other people, too, but the moment I was at his place, he wanted to know if I had £2.00 with me because he needed to buy tobacco. Every few minutes he has a cigarette in his mouth, always smoking away, the whole place stinking of tobacco, ash all over the coffee table, and he has his expensive mobile phone at the pawn shop. He keeps taking mobile phones and other expensive stuff, like laptops, to the pawn shop, and then he's given a bit of money for his stuff, and later, when he has to get his stuff back, he has to pay a lot more. Still, he never learns his lesson. And he's crazy. He's really crazy. Mad.

Insane.

He tells me that this television is spying on him (hmm, maybe he's not that crazy), and that sometimes the people on the TV swear at him and make fun of him.

I listen to him and I say nothing back.

What can I say?

Watched the news on C-N. What a lot of crap. Two dogs barking at one another would have made more sense than the crap I watched.

Lazy Joe was mumbling on the screen, actually mumbling, saying that the unvaccinated are to blame for more cases of the Invisible Enemy virus and he was followed by someone called Dr Leanne who said almost the same thing, almost adding that the people should be forced to take the vaccines.

We're heading towards hell, a hell sponsored by the media, a media controlled by the Invisible Hand. Last days? Or Lost Days? Only time will tell.

Matthew 15:11

Put your trust in the Lord and you will find your true self.

July 18th

I dive into the abyss, eyes open, arms wide open, and, for a moment, I feel as if I'm flying.

I fall, and then I lose myself in the sea, underwater.

I come up for air and find myself inside some cave, an underwater cave, and I must find my way out of there.

I walk in the dark for a few minutes until I see a bit of light. And afterwards I see a cave, a cave going up, a cave made of clouds, not of rocks.

"How can I climb this?" I wonder.

I look up and see someone looking down, some sort of angel, a figure with wings, looking at me.

I stretch my hand up… and then I wake up

I read that a former Human Services Secretary has said that Americans who haven't received the Invisible Enemy's vaccine shouldn't be allowed to work or have access to children, and even have limited access to what places they can go to. There is something wrong with anything that must be forced. Like I've said before, soon they'll come for the unvaccinated. I do fear (and I don't) what's to come. Until then I'll keep on writing.

July 19th

Freedom day has arrived, nightclubs opened at midnight, restrictions have been scrapped, but the media is already selling you fear, saying that cases across UK have soared by 52 per cent and 25 people have died of the Invisible Enemy virus. The media loves the chaos and the fear.

Some of my friends are so scared of going out. They believe every lie they read and see printed and screened.

People are so gullible. Sometimes it looks as if they really want to be misled and lied to. It is almost impossible to make them see anything else. The weaker ones, who are always glued to the screen and post loads online, were the first ones to run to get the vaccine, and afterwards they were quick to change their photos and their status to "I Got the Vaccine" or "Vaccinated" or some other crap, and a few of them stopped talking to me and never accepted my friend request or unfriended me when I told them I wouldn't be getting the vaccine.

The Big Tech and the richest of the lot got together in Sun Valley but to discuss what?

While the world is fighting a global pandemic, and the Invisible Hand is dying to vaccinate everyone, including children, the richest of the lot are planning space trips, even trips to Mars. Meanwhile a war is being fought online as hackers (from China, I read somewhere) try to disrupt the web. And protests are breaking throughout the world.

Joe is sleeping while the Invisible Hand pulls the strings. And Donald is planning a comeback but who is pulling his strings?

He saw a world of hate, a world divided by hate, a world of colours, a world divided because of colours, a world where families were being destroyed because of words, a world of no families, a world where words like father and mother or he and she were slowly being erased by the cruellest of the lot. It was an insane world, a world of insanity, a world of insane words, ruled by fanatics, by families who would keep on growing, powerful families that thought of nothing when destroying the word family. Later, the transformation would arrive; the age when human would merge with the machine. And then the end (of humanity) would arrive. Unless Nature (and the Universe) had something else in store for Humanity. A blast from the sky, maybe? No wonder some billionaires were in a rush to get to space.

Yu sent me some strange texts. In one of them she wrote, "Let me know if you're OK. Even though we don't really speak, I still care about you."

What?

And a few hours later, she wrote, "Are you OK? Let me know if you need anything."

What?

What is she after?

What does she want from me?

I didn't bother to reply.

The truth is I had nothing to say to her.

Last year, when she left me with nothing, I was dying, really dying, dying inside, and no one came to my rescue.

And this year, when I was sick, and later dying again, or almost dying, just hanging by a thread, no one called to ask how I was, certainly not Yu, who completely abandoned me after I left the hospital, and I had such a terrible month that I thought about quitting, give up All, including Life, and now she's asking if I'm OK?

It's too late for that NOW.

Maybe she's the one who's not okay.

Maybe she's coming to the conclusion that she might end up alone lest she change her ways.

The Italian government is now saying that unjabbed people might be banned from being served indoors at restaurants and bars and from entering stadiums. Soon England might say the same thing, followed by the rest of the world. No news from China on this matter. Hmm…

The war against the unjabbed has only just started. Right now, I think I'm the only person who hasn't yet been vaccinated at my workplace, the black sheep, waiting to be shot by those working for the Invisible Hand. But maybe the Invisible Hand is paying me to write this book. After all, they love money. And I need a bit of it, too.

Love?

20ᵗʰ July

Went to the Jesus Centre where I spent some time with Jeremy and a few friends. Ate a sandwich and a banana while in there, drank two cups of juice, and played a game of pool. A lot of unjabbed people there, just enjoying life, trying to stay out of trouble, dreaming of who knows what. Julian arrived later. He got himself a cup of coffee and then went straight to the computer to catch up on the news. Julian sleeps on the streets so he doesn't always has access to a computer, and whenever he can (access a computer) he reads the news, watches a few documentaries on YouTube, and maybe even checks on his emails.

No news of Su. No one knows what happened to her. She's travelling and that's it.

Julian told me that later she might make a brief return to Coventry. She made a few friends here, knows which places to go for a meal, which places are safe, so we might still see her again.

Thursday, 22ⁿᵈ July 2021

Yu is already looking for a new job. She hasn't told me so but when I was at her place I heard her talking to someone on the phone, and a new job was mentioned, and Yu told the other person, who, once upon a time, used to work at our workplace (but he was a lazy bastard, as lazy as Gordon, a character that I've already mentioned in some of my books, a real life character, based on a real life schmendrick), that the first interview went well and that she was told she'll get a second interview and might even get the job, a new job to add to a long list of jobs, and I'm happy for Yu and hope she's happy at this new job, that is if she gets the job, and I'm 100 per cent sure that we'll never get back together, which for me is fine (because she isn't love) because I wouldn't want to go back with her, but I do hope she's happy and that she meets someone else, a good man that will look after her, treat her right, and love her as a man should love a woman, love her faithfully, as I once did.

Life goes on, as does love even if it takes a long break, and there are times when it feels as if love has died –and maybe love dies; maybe the love we felt for someone else dies: it gets killed by harsh words and brutal actions, but we must retain a bit of love inside ourselves, store it right at the bottom of our souls, keep it away from selfish and greedy people, store it well and wait for the right opportunity and the right person to come along before we can let that love out, and even though my love for Yu has died, she'll always have a special place in my heart and I wish her well, and I hope she gets lots of love, just not from me.

As for me, I want to move on, and I want to love again, love with no limits, love the right woman, one woman only. I've always been a one-woman-only type of guy. I don't want affairs, one-night-stands, or to play the part of the stud. That's not for me. I'd rather be a monk, even a celibate monk, than to play the role of the stud.

I left Yu's place a few minutes before 7:00PM, and then took the 14 bus to the city centre. I got off the bus at Allesley Old Road, right in front of the building where me, Yu and the children lived for so many years, and I made my way up the road. The body was tired but the mind needed to be out, see a bit of life, think things over.

Cassandra, Gary and Cassandra's mother were sitting on a plot of land that they bought, and they were happy to see me and invited me to join them; sit down for a while, have a drink and a chat, and so I stayed over for a couple of hours.

Cassandra and Gary are decent people, the kind of people I want as friends.

Cassandra asked me what I thought of Ellie, a friend of hers that I recently met at her house. I told her I really liked Ellie, but I hadn't said a word about her because I thought she was married, but it turns out that Ellie has been divorced for quite a long time, probably more than a decade, and during that time she's been on her own. Ellie's a few years older than me, but I really like her. The first thing I liked about her was her mouth, her lips, the shape of her mouth when she smiles, and I liked her eyes, her hipster way of dressing up. On that night, when I first met Ellie, there was another woman at Cassandra's place, a single woman named Daiyu, and she was also pretty, and I actually met her before Ellie, but, for some reason, the moment I saw Ellie, my eyes (and thoughts) were focused only on her. I made sure to get her a seat right next to me so that I could get to know her better, but I didn't want to sound as if I was being too pushy, plus, at the time, I wasn't really sure if she was single or not, so I ended up not asking that many questions, but when Cassandra told me Ellie's single, I told her straight away that I really like Ellie and that I would like to get to know her better, take her out for coffee or maybe even lunch, maybe to Café Bravo in Earlsdon Street, a nice restaurant close to Ellie's home and only a few minutes away by bus from where I live, a quite café in a quiet area. Cassandra told me she'll try to get more information from Ellie, see what she thought of me, and see if Ellie would like to go out on a date with me. Having someone like Ellie in my life would be fantastic but only time will tell if something will happen between us.

A few friends of Cassandra and Gary stopped by to say hello, and they were the type of people that I like to talk to and spend time with.

I left their place a few minutes past 9:00PM and went straight home. Actually, I lie. I quickly went to Sainsbury's to buy some Huel, fruit, smoked salmon, and dark chocolate, and only then did I went home. Once home, I went straight to bed. I feel asleep with Ellie on my mind. It would be good if she was the one.

This morning, after showering and breakfast, I went straight to Yu's place just so I could look after our children while she went to work. It was a hot morning. Only one person waiting by the bus stop. She was waiting for the 11 bus while I was waiting for the 6A. She was reading the latest book by Siri Hustveidt, a writer that I like, and she almost missed her bus. She got in the bus just as my bus was arriving. The 6A was almost full but a lot of people got off at that stop. I got in the bus, sat behind a young woman reading a book called *all men want to know*. I sat behind her, looked over her shoulder, read a few pages of the book she was reading, and a few hours later I was buying the same book from Waterstones. I also bought a book for my son; *Pokémon Adventures*, volume one, story by Hidenori Kusaka, art by Mato. *All men want to know* was written by Nina Bouraoui.

When I arrived at Yu's place, she was still in her underwear, about to get ready to go to work. I took a look at that voluptuous body in front of me, a body that has gained a bit of weight throughout the ages, but I always loved Yu either way, fat or skinny (but she's not that fat), or I used to love her, but, as I looked at her, I felt almost nothing towards her. She did a big mistake when she asked for the divorce, and then she left me with (almost) nothing, but maybe some things are just meant to happen because if they didn't happen the writer would have no story to tell and life would be a bore, but I liked the boredom, and if my life is always boring so be it. I've had enough "excitement" in my short life to last me for a long time, too many breakups around me, too many divorces, father leaving mother, uncle leaving aunt, aunt leaving uncle, someone else leaving someone else, someone leaving me, too many lies, so much hate, so much bitterness, and I got tired of it all, consumed by it all, saddened by the actions of others, and, from a young age, I decided to be different, to always be faithful to my partner, be a good husband, a good father, but maybe I failed as a husband (but Yu went a bit mad, maybe a bit greedy), and now I have to start again.

A new life, a new wife?

Who knows?

July 23ʳᵈ. 6:00AM. I read Nina Bouraoui at work while waiting for the relief guard to arrive. I write down the names of Yves Navarre, Jean-Louis Bory and Wilhelm Reich, writers I still haven't read, writers whose works I need to check out, followed by the name of Joan Baez, a singer I haven't heard in decades. I hide myself in books and on songs of the past. Or maybe that's wrong. Maybe I find myself in books and songs of the past.

When the relief guard arrives, we exchange a bit of small talk, and afterwards I quickly rush to the city centre. I have to be at Yu's place before she leaves for work so our children won't be left alone, but I'm also hungry and I need some breakfast. A quick stop by McDonald's where I get breakfast and then I slowly chew on my food as I make my way to the bus stop. My body is tired, ready to shut down, but I still have a bus to catch, a short journey to make, a talk on Zoom waiting for me at 8:00AM, and then I have to prepare breakfast for my daughter; my son makes his own breakfast, so it will be close to three hours before I finally manage to get some rest. And even then I'll only manage to get a couple of hours rest, not a couple of hours sleep. But I'm not complaining.

I speak to Ellie on the phone. Cassandra gave her my number and then asked Ellie if it was okay to give me her number, and once I had Ellie's phone number I called her. We arrange a date for Sunday. Our first date. Will she be the one? Is love actually alive, only sleeping? Too early to know, and I still haven't really met Ellie. I saw her once, spoke with her for a few minutes, but we're still strangers.

In the afternoon I take Leaf out to Earlsdon. She wants a cake and a milkshake. I just want to rest. We take the bus. As of yet, I still don't have a car. Yu kept everything, and she's still not happy. She wanted more but isn't everything more than enough?

We go to Café Bravo. In less than two days, if all goes well, I'll be here with Ellie, on our first date. Needless to say, I'm a bit nervous, but maybe she's nervous too. I'll be a gentleman towards her.

Leaf's tired, and we misses the bus home, so I call Yu and ask her if she can give us a lift back to her place. She says okay. She'll be off work in 2 minutes and it only takes a few minutes to get to where we are.

A few minutes later, Yu pick us up. We hardly say a word to one another on the way back to her place, and when we get there she seems to be in a bad mood, a really foul mood, but I don't say a word about it. I quickly grab my things, kiss my children goodbye, and leave. And even though I'm tired, instead of heading straight home, I take the 14 bus to Pool Meadow Bus Station. The city centre is still brimming with life. I bump into Julian and Jeremy near Starbucks. They're waiting for the food van to arrive. I wait with them.

I think of Ellie then. I wonder how she is, who she is, what will be of us. But there's no point on rushing things or thinking too much stuff that still hasn't happened.

Could it be that after all the madness of the past year my life could actually improve? I hope so.

173

I need some changes in my life, someone, love, but I'm not rushing into anything.

July 24th

My first book is out!

I can hardly believe it.

Out on eBook and paperback.

I've published before, only on Amazon Kindle, and it's great to see my book out on paperback. But even though I've published my first book, there's no celebration. Not yet. I've got nowhere to go, no one to see, no... The story of my life for the last few months, but maybe things are finally changing.

I see the book on Amazon, look at its cover, and then I remain where I am, looking at my laptop, wondering where to go, what to do now that I'm finally published. There's only one thing to do. Keep on living. Keep on writing. And wait on better days. Wait on love.

Love... oh, that small word. Such a powerful word. At times, such a hurtful word.

Love, love, love, what have you done to me?

July 25th

A book out yesterday, a date today.

My date with Ellie went well. We went to Café Bravo, then we took her dog for a walk, and later we had tea at her place. And we kissed.

I told her I liked her the moment I saw her, and it is true. There's no reason to lie. There's never a reason to lie when it comes to love, to loving.

The moment I went looking for Jesus, or the minute Jesus took a hold of me and directed me towards Him, my life changed for the better. But I still have a lot to learn, so much to do, so much...

Last year I used to sit outside Holy Trinity Church, and write and cry, and now I attend the services at the same church.

26th

The first copies of my book have been sold. And I met a woman that I like. Maybe, just maybe things will improve.

Tuesday, 27th July

Yu is mad. Really mad. And aggressive. So aggressive.

Yesterday morning, before she went to work, I tried to be the good guy and told her I no longer want to fight or argue. Even though I'm still (a bit) angry with her because of what she did (but maybe it was all for the best – imagine being with her for the rest of my life?), I no longer want to waste my time arguing or waste my thoughts on hate (and to be honest, I don't even want to waste my time with Yu, but for now, because of the children, I must speak to her, spend a few minutes here and there with her), and I thought it would be better for the children if me and her spoke nicely with one another (but once the children are older, I will probably have nothing to do with Yu), and so I said, "Look, I no longer want to fight or argue with you. What happened happened and sooner or later we will both find someone else, remarry or whatever, move on, etc., so let's put everything aside and stop arguing."

Yu said, "You're right. There's so much hate in the world, especially at our workplace where almost everyone is an idiot."

I nodded, and I had to agree with her about what she said about some of our colleagues. But I didn't want to badmouth anyone so I let the subject die. And with that, she left to go to work. I thought that was it (but this is Yu I'm talking about – and she loves to scream), but on that same night, she went berserk because our son Matthew didn't check something online, and she started to scream, and then she told me I should start doing some work at her place, do her garden, fix up a few things at her place, be her slave, unpaid, become her idiot, again, etc., and I thought, "The nerve of her! First she buys a place behind my

175

back, while she's still married to me, leaves me with nothing, and now she wants me to work for her?"

I couldn't help but laugh about it.

Was Yu actually crazy?

The world was spinning at a fast speed, spinning weirdly, making me dizzy, and Yu's screaming was making it all seem like a bad movie. What the hell was I doing there?

The children…

My children.

They needed me.

I need them.

Leaf wanted me to stay the night but I apologised to my daughter and told her it was best if I went home. It breaks my heart not to be able to spend as much time as I can with my children, but I also don't want to spend a lot of time near Yu. I no longer hate her (and I'm repeating myself) (repeat, repent), but I think I will never really like her, not even a bit, or forgive her for what she did to me. (Repeat, repent, forgive.)

I want to move on, find someone else, someone else to love, someone who loves me back, no lies, no deceiving, just an honest relationship.

Love isn't dead. It's hiding from hate, and I must find it.

This morning I told my daughter that soon I want to start dating again, get myself a new girlfriend, a new woman, a new love, and Leaf was okay with it, but she said, "Just make sure she accept us."

The way she said it was so sweet and innocent, and almost scared, sounding as if she was scared that I would forget her once I started to date someone else, and the way she said it really touched me. I felt her pain, the pain of losing a father, and her fears running through me, and as I looked at those innocent eyes that were looking at me, I felt like holding her and never letting go of her. I pulled my daughter close to me and gave her a big hug. And then I said, "Of course. Papa will make sure that whoever I date will always accept you and Matthew. After all, the two of you are my everything."

That was good enough for her.

I emailed someone from the council. I need help, a bit of guidance. I need my own place so that my children can spend more time with me.

Yu has got herself a new job. Another job for the collection. I hope she's happy this time. She only starts in September and she'll be working mainly from home which means that later I might be able to stop working nights. I need a change, a new job. Or maybe remain at my workplace but change my hours.

July 28th

Second date with Ellie. Our first proper date.

Dinner in Earlsdon. Here we go again.

Love, behave.

I hope things work out between me and Ellie. And if they do, I wonder how Yu will feel afterwards.

My life has changed so much in the last few days. I got a book published, had my first date with Ellie, finished another book, and now I'm working on a book that I started ages ago, and once that book is finished I'll send it to a publisher.

I can't stop now.

There's no stopping now.

Monday, 2nd August. I've been so busy with other writing projects and with Ellie that I've forgotten my journal. This journal. This crazy journal turned mad novel. Maybe forgotten is the wrong word.

Because I'm so busy with other things, and because I'm trying to put the final touches to another book so that I can send it to a publisher, I don't really have enough time to write in my journal.

I've been out with Ellie a few times; dinner, long country walks with her dog, and I love spending time with her. We're going slowly with our romance, taking things day by day, and only a few close friends of ours know about it.

I went to see the children on Saturday, after getting only a few hours' sleep. When I got there, it was a few minutes past 1PM. Yu was still in bed, playing on her phone. Flashback of a past life that I have left behind, a cold life spent with Yu. Looking at her, I felt nothing for her. I didn't even want to be there but my children needed me. On the previous night, Leaf texted me from her mother's phone and told me to go and see her on the following day because she missed me. I was so happy to hear my daughter's voice on the phone and to know that she missed me, but I was also sad for being away from her, for not being able to have my children living with me, if only for a few days a week. Maybe one day, G-d willing, I will have my own place, a small home, and my children will be able to spend more time with me. But before that day happens, I will lose so much, time that I will never be able to get back.

Love dies, and afterwards a parent misses so much.

When I got to Yu's place on Saturday, Leaf came running to the door. I saw her through the glass, a big smile on her face. Matthew let me in. He was playing on his laptop. I took a good look at my son. He was growing so fast and was almost my height. Leaf too was playing on her laptop. They were both a bit hungry and there was nothing cooked for them. Yu was laying her lazy fat body in bed, but, in her defence, she did look a bit poorly. She told me she'd taken the second jab for the Invisible Enemy (just so you know, that's the name I've given to the virus of 2020+, a virus that a person isn't even allowed to mention by its name on YouTube – but why?) and she wasn't feeling very well. But it only took her a few seconds to become all bossy towards me (so much for being poorly), and afterwards she told me to cook something for them, but the moment I was in the kitchen, she felt a lot better, and then, magically, she got up, got changed, and told me she was going out. Matthew went out with her because they needed to get some stuff for his camping trip. And then she decided to go to McDonald's and get some lunch for them, nothing for me, but I could still cook and leave dinner ready for them. She returned less than two hours later, or maybe it had gone past two hours, and the first thing she said was, "I hope you didn't cooked too much pasta."

She's always ready to criticise. Always.

I smiled at her. It was a smile that said I pity her. And maybe I still hate her, just a tiny bit, but I don't think I do. Pity, yes, not hate.

Shopping out of the way, she went straight to bed. Straight to her phone.

A flashback of the past, of a life gone past. A cold life. A life I no longer miss.

On Sunday I went out with Ellie for a long walk. As we walked side by side, I felt as if I already knew her, not from this life but from a previous life. Her face looks so familiar. Maybe that's why, when I first saw her at Cassandra's place, I was instantly attracted to her. Could it be that we were a couple in a previous life?

I need a new life, a new start.

Maybe things will improve soon.

Maybe they're already improving.

Before I forget, I must mention that Brie got in touch with me on Facebook a few days ago, or rather she sent me a message which she then deleted. Brie was the last woman I went out with. We went out for a couple of months, maybe a bit longer, but my heart wasn't yet ready to move on.

Brie's a good woman, and I felt bad for breaking up with her, but I couldn't lead her on and give her false hopes. And now that I'm ready to move on, I would like to do it with a new woman, a new face, maybe with someone like Ellie, but only time will tell what will be of us.

Cassio called me on Saturday. He needs money. Always. He always needs money.

He still owes me £30 pounds, and now he wants to borrow ten more. I don't know what he does with his money.

I met him in town this afternoon and lent him the money. He said, "Call me on Tuesday, arrange a time for Wednesday so that I can give you the money straight away, or else I might spend it."

Spend it on what?

Gambling, of course.

Throughout the years, I told him repeatedly to stop gambling but he never listens to me.

And this afternoon I told him that I don't know what time I'll be in the city centre on Wednesday because I'm looking after my daughter but he wasn't really listening.

Cassio tires me out. He really wears me out. In fact, he wears most of his friends out, even his sister, because he never learns from his mistakes.

A few days ago, I spoke to Rute, a friend that me and Cassio have in common, and even she told me that she no longer knows what to do about Cassio. We give him advice after advice, tell him where he's going wrong, how he can improve his life, and we try to direct him towards a better life, but Cassio isn't listening.

He keeps calling his sister in Portugal asking her for money but she can't help him either. And she also needs money for herself, but Cassio can't see that. The problem with people like him is that the more you give him, the more he asks. I really don't know what to do about him. No one does.

August 4th (yes, still 2021)

I went to the city centre with my daughter. I spoke to Cassio early in the morning and we agreed to meet outside Waterstones on Smithford Way around 3PM. I arrived in town a few minutes before 2PM. Me and Leaf wanted to browse through a few shops before going to meet Cassio. The first shop we went to visit was Forbidden Planet on 31 Cross Cheaping, but we had just entered the shop when my phone rang. Straight away, I knew the caller was Cassio. I didn't even had time to greet him because he spoke the moment I answered the call, and he was almost aggressive on the phone, saying, "M÷, where are you? I'm already in town!"

It was two minutes past 2PM. We had agreed to meet at 3PM. I really don't know what Cassio problem is. Is he crazy? I believe so.

I apologised to my daughter and told her we would go and see Cassio first, get my money from him, and then we would return to Forbidden Planet. Leaf said okay. She knows that I'm getting sick of Cassio. He's not a bad man but dealing with him can be very tiring.

Me and Leaf crossed the road, cut through West Orchards Shopping Centre, and when we got to Smithford Way there was no sign of Cassio. Alarm bells started to ring as I thought the worse: "He spent the money gambling. My money. Money that me and my children need for our holidays. And now he's gone home."

We waited by the fountain and a few seconds later I saw Cassio making his way toward us. He couldn't give me all the money that he owes me. He could only give me £20 pounds, and he would give me the other £20 pounds later. But when? And he still owes me an extra £10 pounds which I lent him ages ago but I no longer bother to ask him for that money.

I took the money from Cassio and I thought that was that, and that I could finally enjoy the day with my daughter, but this is Cassio we're talking about, and, with Cassio, everything is craziness, madness, and the disappearance of money. He told me he got a letter from British Gas saying he owes more than five hundred pounds (and I thought, what kind of world is Cassio actually living in?), and then he told me that spirits are spending his electricity, I kid you not, and that's why he owes so much money (and I thought, what kind of mad world is Cassio actually living in?), and he went on and on how his apartment is cursed and spirits live there (and I thought, oh, you already know what I thought).

If I let him talk, we would have been there for a long time, a lot longer than needed, a lot longer than I wanted to be, so I quickly made my excuses and told Cassio I had to go to a few shops with my daughter, eat something with her, and that was it. I don't know when he will give me the rest of the money, but, right there, I didn't care about the money. I just wanted to enjoy the day with my daughter.

Leaf and I spent a few hours in the city centre, looked at some Manga, ate something from McDonald's, and later we paid a visit to Cassandra and Gary. They're such good people, two of the best persons I've met in my life, and Leaf loves them too.

August 5ᵗʰ

Love dies.

It gets killed by the coldness of others, by rejection, unanswered calls, unwritten messages, ghosting, insincerity.

Love dies but M÷ still had faith (faith on love), and so he kept pursuing it, but, bit by bit, no matter how much faith he had, even he was starting to get tired of all the lies and coldness. But there was hope. And there was someone else on the horizon. Could she be love?

Messi is leaving Barcelona.

The end of an era.

I thought he would stay there for a few more years, then move to the States and play there for another couple of years, but that isn't going to happen.

778 games.

672 goals.

305 assists.

35 trophies.

I don't think Barcelona will have another Messi.

I sit on the floor, lotus position, eyes closed.

I need this time, time alone with nothing, time to breathe, time to see the future, time…

I see…

A world of humans making love to machines.

A world…

A world of transhumanists.

A world that is no world.

A world of masks and no love.

A world that is no world.

A world where humans are counted, where mothers are told to abort because it is the right thing to do.

A world that is no world.

A world where humans are counted, and after a certain number, no one is allowed to give birth.

A world where the word father no longer exists.

A world of no grandfathers.

A world where the machine stores the semen and the eggs in factories.

A world that is no world.

A world where the writer no longer exists.

A world devoid of poetry.

A world that is no world.

I see… no love.

August 6th

After my shift ends, I head straight to Yu's place to look after the children. The body is tired but the father can't stop. I make a quick stop at home, change clothes, and then catch the 6A bus to Yu's place. A grey sky, promising rain. In fact, it rains a bit while I'm at the bus stop.

My mind wanders from thought to thought. A song called *Boiler* by Limp Bizkit keeps playing somewhere in the back of my mind, a song whose words now make so much sense. But life goes on. And I can love again. In fact, there is someone else in my life, someone I like, but I'm going slowly this time. She's not in a rush either because she's been hurt too.

I have breakfast at Yu's place but I take my food with me. A few eggs, a slice of bread, a banana, and some barley to drink. And while I'm there, because my body is telling me I need it, I sleep for a couple of hours. As usual, I fall asleep to the sound of Kelly Howell's voice. By the time I wake up, I see that Leaf is still in bed, playing on her phone. I miss this; these quiet moments with my daughter, moments that are so rare now, but one day, G-d willing, both my children will be with me again.

G-d willing, G-d willing…

I keep repeating myself.

Please, Lord…

I get out of bed, say a prayer, wash my hands, followed by another prayer, and another…

A life of prayer is something I've always wanted, a life close to G-d, but, unfortunately, for quite a long time, I lived another life, a sinful life, a life away from G-d. Good thing G-d wasn't away from me. He was there, waiting for me to fall, waiting for me to repent, just so He could take me back in His arms. So now I'm grateful, so grateful for the many chances I've had, and I know I must try harder. And everything starts with prayer.

A life of prayer, so different from the life I've left behind.

After breakfast, me and Leaf go to Earlsdon. I'm meeting Ellie for tea and biscuits and I want for my daughter to meet the woman I love. We wait for the rain to slow down. Then for Leaf to stop watching something on telly. And afterwards my daughter takes her time getting changed. But it's okay. We're not in a rush, and Ellie told me she'll meet me anytime.

Matthew doesn't want to come out. He's too tired from his four days of camping and wants to catch up on his gaming and chat with some friends online. That's fine with me. A short journey on the 14 bus to Carlton Court. The bus stops right in front of the building where I used to live with my children and Yu. Only a few months ago I would cry whenever I walked past the building, but now I no longer miss that place. As a matter of fact, I couldn't see myself living with Yu again. No matter how hard I try, I can't really forgive her. She's moving on with her life, leaving everyone behind, getting rid of people as one gets rid of an old piece of clothing. She only keeps those she can get something from. Everyone else is disposable, even love. She's so cold and so ugly. I can't believe I married her. I can't believe I fell for her lies, for such an ugly soul. But it's okay; I'm planning a new life too. For now, I keep quiet about it, but there will be a time when I no longer will have to be in touch with Yu. For now, because of the children, I speak a little with her, as little as possible, but the Day will come when I no longer will have to address her. And I can't wait for that Day to arrive. But what if she ever needs me? Really need me? What if she's ever in need of a friend? Alone in the dark, in the darkness of the soul? Will I abandon her?

Will I be that cold?

I can't...

I could but I won't.

Leaf and I make our way up Mount Street. We walk past Cassandra and Gary's place. They've been so good to me, almost a shoulder to cry on. They can't even imagine how much they helped me when I was going through my Dark Period. I was dying, really dying, but their friendship and warmness helped me to carry on. G-d put them on my path just at the right time.

I met a few good souls while going through my Dark Period, not many (good souls) but enough. The Lord knew what I needed, whom I needed, and He put those people on my path. And so, Life Goes On.

Love dies, but only briefly, sometimes for a long period of time, and during that time, the loser, the giver, the one who loved too much, feels as if he or she is stuck in a limbo, lost in a Dark Place, and, depending on how much you've loved and how much you've lost, some people feel like quitting, as if they have nothing to live for, but Life Goes On, and some things happen for a reason, whatever that reason is. And quitting is never an option. And it is.

No one knows how the other person really feels when he or she loses it all.

No one knows one's pain.

And sometimes quitting is the only option left, the cure for the pain. And it isn't.

Quitting is never an option, no matter how sad we are, no matter how much we hurt inside, but, looking back, if I relive the pain of the last 16 months, maybe more, I know how those who quit really feel. Losing it all, and having to start again, from scratch, with nothing, isn't easy, and some people don't have the strength to go through it all again.

Love again after losing it all?

To hell with that!

I feel for those who quit.

I understand their pain.

I've been there too.

Every once in a while, I still travel down that road, the road that takes me towards the Dark Path. That's when I get down on my knees and pray. There's someone out there listening to us. Sometimes we aren't listening to Him.

The illusion of movement; we run, and run and run, without ever getting anywhere. Sometimes, instead of running, we need to slow down.

Before I forget, I must add that me and Leaf met a lovely lady while travelling on the 14 bus. We spoke with her for a bit, about Tokyo and Manga because Leaf was reading a Manga book, and the lady said her son lives in Tokyo, and then I found out that she's also a writer and published her first memoir at the age of 83-years old. Her name is Annie Christina Knox and her book is called *Chrissie O.*

"What a coincidence," I said. "I also published my first book recently."

I wrote her name down, and I bought her book on that same day.

We spoke about the various churches in Coventry, and about G-d, Ireland, Tokyo, books, etc. She was a lovely lady to talk to, and I felt then that the Lord was blessing me more every day by sending such good people into my life. I had closed my eyes to the Lord, to faith, and I trusted Man instead of the Creator. Maybe that's where I went wrong.

The moment Ellie arrived at Myrtles, I felt so happy. She brings brightness to my life. Early days but I hope she's the one. I feel as if I already know her, as if I have met her before. Maybe…

At first, Leaf is a bit shy towards Ellie but they quickly become friends. They're both Light, the brightness that my life needs.

The Snake tried to kill Love, but Love is still alive.

The Lord saved me from the Darkness, and then sent Love my way.

When I'm around Ellie, I feel so calm. She brings out the best in me. I become a gentleman, a modern version of Ronald Colman. A dashing hero in a world going out of control, a world controlled by an Invisible Hand. And Ellie becomes my lady, my muse, the love I was looking for.

The love…

The love?

August 7th

Love dies. And then the Snake lies. But the Snake –Yu– never loved me. She took what she needed and then crawled on, swallowing dirt along the way.

This afternoon I went to my old brother-in-law's house to see him and some of the family. My son Matthew went with me. He wanted to see his cousin Bao and to meet his other cousin, Huan, the older brother of Bao. Matthew's already friends with Bao but he still hasn't met Huan.

Tan, Yu's older brother, was happy to see us, and he had told me on the previous day that Mei, his younger sister, and Ma, his younger brother, would also be coming. In way, it was a family reunion, minus Yu. No one can stand Yu, which I find a bit sad because, unless things change, one day Yu will find herself alone. But just because she isn't in touch with her family it doesn't mean that my children shouldn't see their family too.

Before I came to Tan's place, I asked Yu if she could give us a lift. She has a car, a car that used to be mine too, but she went berserk when I asked her for a lift, and she started to shout, which is quite the norm nowadays with her, and she said she wasn't a bloody cab driver, and, blah blah blah; she was shouting so much that I didn't even heard what she was saying; she did mention something about me not giving her a lift if she needed, and I had to remind her that she was the one with the car, and she started mocking me, something she has done quite often in the past, and said, "Oh, poor you."

The mocking is never nice, but, you know, I'm kind of moving on, and Yu's behaviour is getting tiring, not to mention repetitive, a bit like me when I write, and I simply ignored her. For a brief moment I did felt like swearing at her, tell to her face what I really thought of her, but she bores me now, and I no longer want to waste oxygen on her. No one does and that's why she's alone.

She did drop me and Matthew halfway so I can't complain, but everything with her is shouting, shouting, shouting, and I'm getting too old for it. I never thought I would say this (and I'm repeating myself), but the less I see of Yu, the better it is.

She's a petty soul and I no longer want to write about her. But I must. For now, she's part of the story. She's the snake in my garden. She ate the apple and put the blame on me. And everyone believed her lies. Or some people did, but after a while the liar gets trapped in their own lie, and then what? Then it's loneliness, the gnashing of teeth, sorrow, regret, and the fall of the pride.

Anyway, me and Matthew walked half the way, a bit of a long walk but the body needs a bit of exercise, not to mention fresh air and sunshine, and while we were making our way to Tan's place, Matthew told me he's sick of his mother, sick of living with her, most of all, he's sick of the shouting, of her rash decisions. He then told me about Colin, the guy Yu went out for a few weeks, and Matthew actually liked Colin; he told me Colin was good to him and Leaf, and whenever they went out, Colin always paid for everything and he took them to loads of places, but neither Matthew or Leaf know why Yu broke up with Colin. It's not good for the children to see these things; to see their mother bringing a man home, sleep with him for a few weeks, and then, all of a sudden, break up. What is going through Yu's head? No one knows.

I didn't know what to say.

My son told me he would move in with me when I have my own place. That's good news but when will I have my own place? Soon, I hope.

We had lunch at Tan's house and it was good to see the family together. Matthew played with his cousins while I spoke with Mei for a long time. She has gotten prettier with age. She's always been pretty but now she's even prettier. Later at night, when I was already at work, Mei messaged me on Facebook and apologised for everything that Yu did to me, and I told her not to worry about it and that there was no need for her to apologise for her sister's mistakes.

A lot was said about Yu at Tan's house, mostly bad stuff, but I won't bother to write about it here. And I don't like it when other people speak badly about Yu. She might not be perfect, but neither am I, and neither is her family, especially those who badmouthed her. But they're my family too, and, perfect or not, every single one of them will always have a special place in my heart.

What happened between Yu and I had to happen, and now there's no need for me to think about it, or even write about it.

After this novel is finished, I'm going to write a big sci-fi novel.

Love dies, or so we think, and we take a break from it; a break from love, and then, when we least expect it, love resurfaces, and it has the face of another, a prettier face, maybe older, and this time you know love won't die until one of you dies, and even then, after one of you dies, love will wait for the other one on the Other Side.

I was wrong when I said that love is pain.

Love isn't pain.

Love is immortality.

Thursday, 12th August

Cassio called me.

Oh no!

He needs money.

Oh no!

Twenty pounds.

Oh brother!

He still owes me twenty pounds but he needs to borrow twenty more.

Dear me.

I tell him I can't lend him the money. Not today.

I tell him I need to go to the bank, check my bank account. Basically, I lie, but I'm tired of always lending him money. And he still owes me money. When will he pay me that money?

His life is a disaster.

I don't know what will be of him one day.

And what will be of me?

August 15th

I'm in love. Again.

Oh no.

I hope this is it. Again.

Here we go…

As weird as this may sound, I feel as if I have met her before, somewhere else, in another time, another era, another age, maybe in another life.

I've told Yu about my new love, about Ellie. I wanted for her to hear it from me and not from someone else. She didn't say a word about it. What could she say? That was a few days ago.

And now I'm waiting outside Holy Trinity Church, waiting on Ellie, waiting on love.

I thought love had died.

I thought I was about to die.

Instead I was given another chance.

And so I wait.

Someone that I know is crying while waiting for the food bank people to arrive. She came over to where I was, sat down, said hi, and, seconds later, she was crying.

Why?

Because of love, that's why.

Because love hurts.

Because being in love hurts.

Because being dumped by the one you love hurts.

Because seeing the person that you love move on-move in with someone else hurts.

That's why she's crying.

I don't know what to tell her.

I tell her that things will be alright.

What?

What am I saying?

I tell her that, even if it takes a long time, things will be alright.

What?

Shut up, M÷.

I tell her...

Basically I lie.

But what can I say?

The truth?

That she will be in pain for a long time?

That she will cry and cry and cry until she begs to die?

I can't say that, can I?

Love is pain.

Her man, or the man she loves as he's no longer her man, is also at the food bank. And his new woman is here too.

And they're holding hands and smiling and laughing and…

And someone else is crying.

I told you: love is pain.

I sent a message to Brie on Yom Kippur, a message where I apologised for what I did to her.

Brie's a good woman, a decent woman, an angel that was there when I needed someone, a woman that waited for me, that loved me and then watched me leave, but, back then, I couldn't love.

After moving away from my children, I couldn't love.

I was incapable of loving anyone.

All I could do was cry.

For months, I cried.

For months, I died.

I hope Brie forgives me for the wrong I did to her, which reminds me that, if I want to be forgiven, I too must forgive.

Epilogue

When he lost everything, or what he thought as everything (but the truth is we come into this world with nothing and leave with nothing – but the actions of the flesh), he retreated into a dark corner, a place he'd been before, a bad place, a place where weaker souls than his had been to, and, in there, he found it hard to breathe, and he couldn't see past the despair of his soul, but as he navigated through those troubled waters, through an ocean of despair and tears, an ocean that was calling out for his blood, he dig deep inside himself for strength, a strength he thought he didn't have, a strength he never knew he possessed, and he found something in there, a glimpse of hope, something that could help him get through those troubled waters, strength to swim through that dark ocean, only a bit of strength, just enough to get through the ocean (and live to see another day). He saw that the world is a lie: reality itself is a lie, an illusion, and one day the body will turn to dust, and then becomes nothing, but the spirit travels on, the journey starts now, here, there, somewhere, wherever you are, at the last breath, and no one knows where and how it will end. But the first steps for the journey starts with the body, with the flesh, with prayer, with faith.

With Love.

Peter Raposo is the author of dUST. He lives somewhere in England, in a room surrounded by books, notepads and pens.

Printed in Great Britain
by Amazon

81425434R00112